The Karate Kid  Part III

The Karate Kid
Part III

COLUMBIA PICTURES Presents A JERRY WEINTRAUB Production   A Film By JOHN G. AVILDSEN

"THE KARATE KID PART III" Starring RALPH MACCHIO   NORIYUKI "PAT" MORITA

Music by BILL CONTI   Co-Producer BROOKS ARTHUR   Executive Producer SHELDON SCHRAGER

Produced by KAREN TRUDY ROSENFELT   Written by ROBERT MARK KAMEN   Based on Characters Created by ROBERT MARK KAMEN

Produced by JERRY WEINTRAUB   Directed by JOHN G. AVILDSEN

A COLUMBIA PICTURES RELEASE

point

The Karate Kid III
Part

A novelization by B.B. Hiller.
Based on a motion picture
written by Robert Mark Kamen.
Based on characters created by Robert Mark Kamen.

SCHOLASTIC INC.
New York Toronto London Auckland Sydney

ISBN 0-590-43043-2

12 11 10 9 8 7 6 5 4 3 2   9/8 0 1 2 3/9

Printed in the U.S.A.   01

First Scholastic printing, July 1989

This book is dedicated to
Emmons B. Hiller

Chapter 1

"I think it's time to get back to my training," Daniel LaRusso said over his shoulder to his friend, Mr. Miyagi. "This luggage is getting heavier with every step I take!" The two were walking through Los Angeles International Airport — the final step of their long journey home from Okinawa. Not only were they each carrying large suitcases, but Daniel was overloaded with souvenirs from their visit.

Even Mr. Miyagi was straining under the weight of his luggage — and the souvenirs Daniel had asked him to carry.

"Strange your mother not here to meet us, Daniel," Mr. Miyagi said, shifting a carryall from one shoulder to the other. "Sure you told her the right flight?"

Daniel stopped for a minute and checked his ticket. "Right flight," Daniel assured him. "But I think I told her the wrong day. I forgot about crossing the international date line. I told her we'd arrive tomorrow morning." Daniel looked at Mr. Miyagi. "She loves surprises," Daniel said.

"Hope so," said Mr. Miyagi.

Daniel was more than a little annoyed with his mistake. The flight from Tokyo had been long and tiring. This was no time to be trying to find a cab to take them all the way to Reseda. This was a good time to relax in the backseat of his mother's car. His eyes scanned the passenger pickup area hopefully, but there was no sign of her.

Daniel and Mr. Miyagi left the airport. As they walked out, a man entered. They did not see him, but if they had they would have known who he was. It was John Kreese.

Kreese was the instructor at the Cobra Kai Karate School, and while both Daniel and Mr. Miyagi loved karate, there was nothing they loved about Cobra Kai. When Daniel had first moved to California ten months ago, he'd gotten into a fight with one of Kreese's students at the Cobra Kai *dojo*. As a result, Mr. Miyagi, who was Daniel's friend and karate trainer, or *sensei*, had found himself at odds with Kreese. Daniel had beaten his opponent almost a year ago at the All-Valley Karate Championship. But that hadn't been the end of it. Kreese seemed to think that Daniel's defeat of his student was a personal insult to him. In retaliation, Kreese attacked Mr. Miyagi in the parking lot after Daniel's victory. Mr. Miyagi had won the fight and humiliated Kreese. Daniel liked to think that that meant the end of the conflict, especially since so much time had passed, but he knew that these things had a way of coming back. Again and again.

Kreese headed toward one of the departure

gates. Meanwhile, Daniel and Mr. Miyagi continued to search for Daniel's mother.

"Daniel-san," Mr. Miyagi said finally. "Since mother not here, suggest you use blocking technique."

Daniel bowed somberly at Mr. Miyagi and then thrust out his left arm as if to parry a karate punch. A cab driver spotted the waving arm and came to a screeching halt. Daniel grinned at Mr. Miyagi.

"Where to?" the driver asked the two of them.

"Home!" Daniel announced, tossing his suitcase in the trunk and packing Mr. Miyagi's luggage in there as well.

Chapter 2

Daniel and Mr. Miyagi settled themselves into the backseat of the taxi for the final step of their long journey. They stared out of the cab's windows at the lush California countryside as they headed through the Los Angeles suburbs toward their home.

California had been home to Mr. Miyagi for more than forty years. For Daniel, it had been home for less than one year. He and his mother had moved to Reseda from New Jersey, and Daniel could hardly believe how much had happened to him since then. He and his mother rented an apartment in a run-down building. The best thing about their new home was that Mr. Miyagi was the handyman there. He and Daniel had become friends when the old man had taken Daniel on as his personal karate student.

Daniel was learning karate from Mr. Miyagi the same way that Mr. Miyagi had learned it from his father, who, in turn, had learned it from Mr. Miyagi's grandfather. Mr. Miyagi claimed that the knowledge had been handed down from father to son for more than twenty generations — in fact, ever since a Miyagi had brought the knowledge to Okinawa from China more than 400 years earlier. Daniel suspected that the story had been somewhat embellished over the decades, but it was nevertheless clear that the Miyagi family knew what they were talking about when it came to karate.

"Turn left here," Mr. Miyagi said to the cab driver. "Then look to right for pink stucco archway and coconut palms."

"Hey, there it is, Mr. Miyagi!" Daniel said excitedly, his eyes alighting on the faded pink of the building's exterior. "Isn't it great to be home? Doesn't it look great?"

Daniel stuck his head out the window to watch as they approached the building, but something was wrong. The archway was gone. A front-end loader with a backhoe was parked in its place. A large moving van was loading up in front of the building, and Mrs. Milo, a rather eccentric lady who lived in apartment 114, was standing by the curb.

"What are you two clowns doing in my cab?" Mrs. Milo demanded.

"Your cab? We just came from the airport," Daniel told her.

"I thought this was the cab I ordered," she said, stepping back while Daniel and Mr. Miyagi climbed out and removed their bags. Mr. Miyagi paid the driver. Daniel was going to ask Mrs. Milo why she'd ordered a cab and whose belongings were being loaded into the moving van when he spotted a billboard by the entrance gate to the building. It read:

5

"Mrs. Milo, what's going on here?" Daniel asked, stunned. The front-end loader, the moving van, and Mrs. Milo's taxi were beginning to add up to a very unpleasant welcome.

"What does it look like?" Mrs. Milo responded. There was disgust in her voice. "Progress," she explained. Then she added, "I got a message for you from your mother." She turned to Mr. Miyagi. "Didn't I tell you that bum would sell the place? Didn't I tell you your job wasn't safe, huh?"

Daniel didn't like the sound of anything he was hearing, and he was beginning to get the feeling he wasn't going to like the rest of what Mrs. Milo had to say, but he had to know what it was. "What's the message?" he asked.

"What message?" Mrs. Milo asked, blinking her eyes in confusion.

"The one from my mother," Daniel explained patiently.

"Oh, she said you should call her collect at your Uncle Louie's."

"Uncle Louie in New Jersey?" Daniel asked in surprise.

"You got an Uncle Louie anyplace else?" she asked.

"I don't think so."

"Then why confuse the issue?"

The look on Mrs. Milo's face made it clear to Daniel that that was all the information he was going to get from her.

6

Then, another cab pulled up to the curb. The driver stepped out and took the woman's bag. She opened the rear door and climbed in.

"Mrs. Milo," Mr. Miyagi said before the cab pulled away. "Where off to?"

"I'm moving back to Parsippany," she told him.

"Parsippany?" Mr. Miyagi said.

"Where progress is still a dirty word," she said, rolling up her window to enjoy the air-conditioning. Then, just before the driver put the car in gear and pulled away from the curb, Mrs. Milo's window rolled down again. "Be careful," she told them. "They're tearing the dump down." The window slid back up. The cab made a U-turn and headed for the airport.

Daniel picked up his suitcase. "I think we'd better get to a phone," he told Mr. Miyagi.

"*Hai*," Mr. Miyagi agreed in Japanese.

Chapter 3

The next few hours were very busy for Daniel and Mr. Miyagi. Though they had hoped to spend the time unpacking and catching up on the sleep they'd lost during their transpacific flight, they actually spent most of it on the phone and then packing.

A call to the apartment office verified that the building was being torn down. Mrs. Milo was, in fact, the last tenant to leave. Mr. Miyagi's job was being terminated along with the building, and he had to get his belongings out of the building workshed as soon as possible.

When Daniel talked with the manager, he learned that his mother had stored their few belongings at Mr. Miyagi's house on the other side of town and, once again, got the message that he was to call his mother collect at Uncle Louie's. The manager even had the phone number.

While Mr. Miyagi tended to his collection of miniature trees — bonsai — Daniel called his mother. She answered on the first ring. It had been almost two months since he'd talked to her, and it was great just to hear the sound of her voice — but not the news she had.

"Your Uncle Louie had a heart attack," she said. "It happened last week. He's doing okay now, but I'm his only family and he needs me."

She explained that she was going to have to stay there for a while, and she asked Mr. Miyagi if Daniel could stay with him and start college while she took care of her uncle.

"Don't worry about anything, Mrs. LaRusso," Mr. Miyagi assured her. "I take good care of Daniel. You just worry about Uncle Louie."

Although Daniel was worried about Uncle Louie and wished he could be with his mother, he was excited about the prospects of staying with Mr. Miyagi. In some ways he and Mr. Miyagi made an odd pair. Daniel had just graduated from high school, and Mr. Miyagi was almost old enough to retire. Daniel had been born in New Jersey; Mr. Miyagi's birthplace was Okinawa. Daniel quickly got excited about things, both good and bad. In contrast, Mr. Miyagi never seemed to be affected by events. He was always calm and assured. In spite of these things, they were close friends.

"No problem," Mr. Miyagi told Daniel's mother on the phone. "You welcome," he said and then he handed the phone to Daniel.

"Yeah, Mom? Are you sure you don't need me?" Daniel didn't like to think of his mother taking care of Uncle Louie all by herself.

"Yeah, I'm sure," she told him. "You stay with Mr. Miyagi and start college. Oh, I can't believe it,

Mr. College Man. When's registration?"

"Next week," Daniel told her.

"So when's Kumiko coming?" she asked. Kumiko was a girl Daniel had met in Okinawa. They had made plans together for her to come to the United States to study ballet, and be with Daniel, but their plans had fallen through.

"She's not," Daniel said. "She got accepted to a dance company in Tokyo. She's going there instead."

"Oh, honey," Mrs. LaRusso said, understanding. "Disappointed, huh?"

"Yeah, but that's life, I guess. I'll survive." Daniel played with the phone cord, thinking about Kumiko, and sighed a little. It seemed that it was easy for him to fall in love, but hard to keep his girlfriends for long.

"I'm sure you'll do more than survive," Mrs. LaRusso said. "Just wait until you meet some of the coeds and — uh-oh. Uncle Louie's calling me. I've got to go. Uncle Louie says hi. Love you."

"Love you, too," Daniel said and then hung up the phone.

Mr. Miyagi had moved all of his tools and most of the bonsai into his pickup truck. Daniel carried a bonsai out the door to the truck, where Mr. Miyagi was tending to the other trees. Although some of them were hundreds of years old, they were only a few inches tall and were quite delicate. It would do them no good to be tossed around in the back of the truck. Mr. Miyagi secured them carefully.

He took the tree from Daniel and packed it with

the others. Then the two friends returned to the shed for the last load.

It was sad to listen to the familiar squeak of the screen door and know it was the last time they would hear it. The sunlight filtered through the dingy windows into the darkened workroom, casting a sad light on the emptiness. Without a word, Mr. Miyagi picked up the last two trees and handed one to Daniel. He turned to leave. Then he paused and took a final look.

Daniel looked, too, knowing that the room held many years of memories for Mr. Miyagi. It seemed very sad that it was coming to such an abrupt ending. For thirty years, Mr. Miyagi had been repairing the plumbing and electricity in the building, coaxing years out of the dilapidated equipment. The old man had repaired generations of bicycles and skateboards, fed pets, and watered plants for vacationing tenants. Daniel felt the three decades of recollections in the dim room as he watched a moment of sadness pass across Mr. Miyagi's face.

"Time to go, Daniel-san," Mr. Miyagi said, turning to open the door. A gentle breeze entered the room, as if to cleanse it of its memories. The wind chimes sang a farewell. Mr. Miyagi sighed.

"You okay, Mr. Miyagi?" Daniel asked.

"Just remembering," Mr. Miyagi said.

Daniel understood. There was nothing he could say about the past, but he had an idea about the future. "So, what are you going to do now?" he asked.

"Don't know. Retire, I guess," Mr. Miyagi said.

"Ever think about opening a bonsai store?" Daniel asked.

Mr. Miyagi looked at him in surprise. Daniel suspected that Mr. Miyagi had thought about it many times. Mr. Miyagi confirmed it. "In my dreams, Daniel-san," he said. "In my retirement."

"Well, what do you call this?" Daniel asked.

"Call it time to go," Mr. Miyagi said matter-of-factly, pointing to the truck.

While Daniel stowed the last bonsai in the truck bed, Mr. Miyagi returned to his workroom's doorway a final time. Daniel noticed that he barely looked back into the room. He simply removed the wind chimes and then shut the door tightly. He didn't bother to lock it behind him. After all, there was nothing there to steal, except memories.

Chapter 4

Daniel was glad to see Mr. Miyagi's house when they arrived. It meant the end of a long journey, but it also seemed to Daniel to be the beginning of something. When they'd left the South Seas Apartments, they'd left Daniel's memories as well as Mr. Miyagi's. Many things were now part of the past, including Daniel's difficult adjustment to California, his bouts with the Cobra Kai students, his girlfriends Ali and Kumiko, his trip to Okinawa, his high school days. But what lay ahead?

The question nagged at Daniel while he helped Mr. Miyagi unload the truck. He took his suitcase and souvenirs into the room Mr. Miyagi had built for him at the back of the house, overlooking the Japanese garden that was hidden from the outside world by a tall, strong fence Daniel had painted himself. He gazed out at the sanctuary and thought about the next day and the ones that would follow it. College? Studies? Classes? Was he really ready for college? he asked himself. He wasn't sure of the answer.

Daniel was a good student. He'd done well enough all through high school, both in New Jersey and Reseda. When he'd graduated, all his mother could talk about was that he was going to college. She'd been saving for years so that he could have the money to go. He'd be the first in his family. It meant everything to his mother.

Daniel wanted to go to college, eventually, but he wasn't sure he wanted to go right now. So many things had happened to him in such a short time that he wondered if it might not be a better idea to take a break and start college at the next semester. Starting college late would mean he'd have to find something else to do until then. He could get a job. After all, Mr. Miyagi was out of work now, and somebody was going to have to earn some money so they could eat. But what kind of job could he get?

Then Daniel's mind wandered back to his earlier conversation with Mr. Miyagi. He thought about school. He thought about money. He thought about Mr. Miyagi. He thought about bonsai trees.

Mr. Miyagi had an amazing skill with the little trees. He'd study a bonsai for hours before he began clipping it. He seemed to know exactly how he wanted the tree to grow and exactly what he'd have to do to make it grow that way. He never tired of his work with any plants, but especially with the bonsai. Along with karate, it was a skill Mr. Miyagi's father had given him and a love he had instilled in him.

As Daniel thought about things, an idea began

to develop in his mind. Then, without a doubt, Daniel knew how he wanted to spend the next few months, and his first year's tuition.

He quickly stowed his clothes on the shelves Mr. Miyagi had built for him in his room, and returned to help Mr. Miyagi finish unloading his truck.

"Hey, Mr. Miyagi," he began, carrying two bonsai carefully into the house. "I've been thinking about the bonsai shop idea. You already have all the stock you could need," he said pointing to the little trees that covered every surface in the house. "How hard could it be?"

"Probably not very hard, Daniel-san," Mr. Miyagi said. "*If* I had money for a lease, rent, deposit, and shop renovations. However, since I now appear to be out of work, money is in very short supply."

"No, it's not," Daniel said. Then, he pulled a wad of cash out of his pocket. It was the money he'd won on a bet when they'd been in Okinawa. Although it had been a foolish bet, it had turned out to be a profitable one. Daniel held enough money in his hand to pay for a full semester of college, or maybe something even better.

Mr. Miyagi's face became stern at the sight of the money. "Thank you, Daniel-san," he said solemnly. "But that is not money."

Daniel looked at the wad as if to examine it. He sniffed at it. "Looks like money to me. Smells like money," he said.

"Smells like college education to me," Mr. Miyagi reminded Daniel.

When Daniel had won the cash, they'd both

agreed that it would be earmarked for tuition, but now Daniel's mind was racing.

"I've got this idea, Mr. Miyagi — " he began.

"No ideas, Daniel-san. Discussion is closed."

Mr. Miyagi took the money, rolled it up again carefully, and stuffed it back into Daniel's pocket.

"Just like that?" Daniel asked. Although he had expected Mr. Miyagi to argue with him, he'd thought the old man would at least hear him out. He hadn't expected his generous offer to be rebuffed at the very beginning. "I mean, what about your dream? Are you just going to forget about it?"

"For now," Mr. Miyagi said.

"Mr. Miyagi, no offense," Daniel countered, "but I think if you miss the train now, there won't be another one for a long, long time." Daniel thought he would score a point with that.

"Then I take a bus," Mr. Miyagi said calmly.

Mr. Miyagi had patience, Daniel knew that. The man knew how to wait for just the right moment to make his move, but it seemed to Daniel that there were times when a little bit of patience was too much. After all, when could the man possibly have another opportunity like this one?

"Why take a bus if you can fly?" Daniel asked, but he got no answer. Carefully and patiently Mr. Miyagi returned to his task, unloading the final bonsai and carrying it into his home.

Daniel watched and thought. He knew what he wanted to do. He just had to figure out how to do it.

Chapter 5

It took Daniel a week to work everything out. He was certain Mr. Miyagi didn't know what he'd done and he was equally certain his friend would object strenuously. He was even more certain that, in the end, Mr. Miyagi would agree that Daniel had done the right thing.

When Daniel arrived home, he found Mr. Miyagi in the kitchen cooking dinner for the two of them.

"How was fishing?" he asked casually, hiding a black lacquer scroll box behind his back.

"We are about to find out," Mr. Miyagi said, pointing to the frying pan where the day's catch was browning. "How was first day of college?"

This was it.

"Uh, I didn't go to college," Daniel said, suddenly nervous.

Mr. Miyagi turned to him. "What?" he demanded.

Hastily Daniel offered him the scroll box. "May all your dreams come true," he said.

"What's this?" Mr. Miyagi asked, staring at the box, but not taking it.

"Only one way to find out," Daniel said sensibly.

Mr. Miyagi wiped his hands on his apron and took the scroll box. He removed the lid. Inside, a long legal document was all rolled up. He took it out, unrolled it, and looked at it in confusion.

"A lease?" he asked, with surprise in his voice.

Daniel smiled proudly. "Yes, a lease — to your new bonsai store. Congratulations."

Mr. Miyagi read the document: " . . . one month security, two months rent — "

"With enough left over for renovations, if we're careful," Daniel finished, producing a much-reduced wad of cash from his pocket.

"Daniel-san, I cannot accept this," Mr. Miyagi said.

"But it's your dream. Why not?" Daniel asked.

"Because money in pocket was to pay for your college, not my dream."

Daniel had expected this and was prepared. "Listen, Mr. Miyagi," he said. "I know me. I can't take courses just to take courses. I'll get bored and once that happens, it's bye-bye college. Look, I'll take the year off, work in the shop, and think about what I want to do. I've been going to school nonstop since I was five. I could use a break."

"I don't know, Daniel-san," Mr. Miyagi said.

"I do know," Daniel said. "Let me show you something. Come on." He motioned toward the truck.

"What about fish?" Mr. Miyagi asked sensibly.

"They're not going anywhere. Come on," he said, handing Mr. Miyagi his cap.

Finally Mr. Miyagi turned off the flame under the fish, donned the cap, and followed Daniel out the door.

Daniel drove the truck, following the twisting roads around the town's center, past the old train station and then, finally, across the tracks. There was a short block of retail stores outside of the main section of town. Daniel pulled the truck up in front of one of them.

"You know, you just can't wait for dreams to come true," he told Mr. Miyagi. "Sometimes you've got to go out and work for them."

He turned off the engine and opened the door. Proudly he led Mr. Miyagi to his dream. Daniel had the key the rental agent had given him. He jiggled it in the lock, trying to get the old tumblers working.

"So, is this the opportunity of a lifetime or what?" he said, pushing at the door to open it. "The landlord said the neighborhood's up-and-coming. I mean, we're in on the ground floor. See, there's a pottery shop that just opened across the street. Maybe we can get some special planters for the trees. It's going to be great. Wait until you see inside."

The door gave, swinging open on squeaky hinges. Daniel entered first and fumbled around until he found the wall light switches. The bare bulbs illuminated Mr. Miyagi's dream.

There was a single large room, filled with the

debris of a fruit-packing plant. The walls were lined with shelves, and the floors were scattered with broken fruit cartons.

Mr. Miyagi's face showed no emotion. Daniel wanted him to see the possibilities because he knew that as soon as that happened, they could begin to make his dream come true. Mr. Miyagi had done so much for Daniel in the last year. Daniel just wanted the chance to do something in return.

"I calculated all our costs for the first year," he explained, taking some sheets of paper out of his jacket pocket. "Overhead, rent, renovation costs. The landlord said we can use anything in here — like all this wood — so we've got eighty percent of our material for free." He handed the list to Mr. Miyagi and then picked up some of the old fruit cartons. "See, this can be a stand and a counter. Over there, we can have a bonsai hospital — you know, in case any of the little guys get sick?" He looked at Mr. Miyagi for some sign of approval, but it wasn't there yet. "I'll work for free until we get going, then you can pay me back. I even thought of a name for the place, 'Mr. Miyagi's Little Trees.' Great idea, huh?" Still there was no reaction from Mr. Miyagi. Daniel went on. "I know you can make it work. If anybody can, you can," he said.

Wordlessly Mr. Miyagi scanned Daniel's list and calculation of expenses. Then he pulled the lease out of his pocket and began examining it closely. Daniel didn't want to interrupt, but he couldn't wait, either. He just *had* to know what Mr. Miyagi was thinking.

"What? Did I forget something?" Daniel asked.

Mr. Miyagi handed him the lease. He also handed him a pen. "Your name. You forgot to put your name on lease next to mine. Partner."

Daniel could barely believe it, but he'd been right and then some. Not only was Mr. Miyagi accepting his gift, loan, really, but he wanted Daniel to be his partner. Joyously he added his name to the lease and signed it. He returned the document to Mr. Miyagi for his signature. Very carefully, Mr. Miyagi signed his name with Japanese characters.

Daniel grinned, thrilled. "This is great!" he said, looking over the complete document. Then, in a rush of excitement, he turned to give Mr. Miyagi a high five or a bear hug, but he was stopped cold, for as he turned, Mr. Miyagi bowed very politely, and very deeply.

"Oh, right," Daniel said, almost embarrassed. He wiped the grin off his face and dropped his hands to his sides. Then, in return, he bowed to Mr. Miyagi very politely and very deeply. That was the right way to treat a business partner.

Chapter 6

The next week was a very busy one for the partners of "Mr. Miyagi's Little Trees." They had to clean and paint the interior of the shop, reinforce the shelving, and create a counter. Mr. Miyagi's years as a handyman stood him in good stead, especially the experience he'd had making dilapidated plumbing and electricity work for the tenants of the old apartment house. Now, however, he was working for himself and Daniel. Using as little of Daniel's spare cash as possible, they began to transform the fruit-packing plant into a bonsai shop.

As Daniel had pointed out, Mr. Miyagi had a lot of bonsai of his own, but they both knew that they'd need more. Until some cash came into the business, they were going to have to find them and create them on their own. After a week of working indoors at the shop, they decided to take a day off and go hunting for likely prospects for bonsai in the nearby woods.

Mr. Miyagi led the way through the piney forest, armed with a shovel and a sharp pair of eyes. Daniel followed, carrying bags and a collection case for their samples.

"Ah-ha! Daniel-san. This is a good one," he said, kneeling down by a four-inch sapling. Daniel knelt down on the other side and studied the little plant. It was an evergreen — probably a cedar, Daniel thought — but it was so young it didn't even have any branches. It looked like a little bottle brush.

"You really see a bonsai here?" Daniel asked skeptically.

"*Hai*," Mr. Miyagi said, digging carefully around the plant. When he took the growth out of the ground, he wrapped the root ball in a moistened towel and protected the moisture with a plastic bag. Then he placed the tree carefully in the collection case Daniel carried for him.

Daniel tried to see what Mr. Miyagi had seen in the sapling. "Where do you see the bonsai?" he asked.

Mr. Miyagi stood up and began searching the forest floor for more trees. "Look inside," he told Daniel.

Daniel stood up, too. He glanced around and saw some underbrush behind him. He parted the branches and bent down as if to look inside. "Hello? Anybody else in there?" he asked, teasing Mr. Miyagi.

Mr. Miyagi wasn't in a teasing mood. "Inside *you*," he told Daniel. "Same place your karate comes from."

This didn't make sense to Daniel. Everything he knew about karate, he'd learned from Mr. Miyagi.

Everything he knew about bonsai, he'd learned from Mr. Miyagi. "But my karate comes from you," he said to his *sensei*.

"Only root of your karate comes from me. Like true bonsai, choose own way to grow. Because root is strong. You choose own way to do karate same reason."

"But I do it your way," Daniel reminded him.

"And one day you will do it own way," Mr. Miyagi said with a finality that left Daniel wondering. However, he had no time to wonder then, for Mr. Miyagi began walking very quickly to a glade where they found several other trees that seemed to Daniel to be unlikely candidates. Mr. Miyagi was pleased with them, though, and that was enough for Daniel.

Because the forest was several hours from Reseda, Daniel and Mr. Miyagi had decided to make a camping trip of it and had established a campsite where they'd pitched their tent and built a temporary fireplace. It was near a crystal-clear stream, bringing icy water from the mountains, and it overlooked the Pacific Ocean from atop a breathtakingly beautiful palisade. It was stunning in its craggy glory, and at this time of year, in the middle of the week, they had the forest and the palisade to themselves. Mr. Miyagi had even made Daniel bring karate equipment so he could get back to his training as he'd been wanting to do.

"Mr. Miyagi," Daniel began as they walked back toward the campsite, their collection case completely filled with potential bonsai. "How come we don't do karate like other people? You know: You count, I punch?"

"Parrots can count, Daniel-san," Mr. Miyagi answered. "Don't need me for that. True karate like true bonsai. If strong root, tree is free to choose own best way to grow. Same karate. Miyagi give you strong root. You're free to choose own way to grow."

"But our bonsai aren't free to choose. We tell them how to grow with our clippers," Daniel reminded him.

"Our bonsai are not true bonsai. True bonsai grow wild. Only nature tell how to grow. True bonsai, natural bonsai, very rare."

"Ever see any?" Daniel asked in surprise. He'd never heard of such a thing as a natural bonsai.

"In Okinawa," Mr. Miyagi told him. "Here, I only know of one."

"What did it do? Immigrate?" Daniel joked.

"*Hai*, with me. Only thing Miyagi take when left Okinawa. Remind me of home. One natural bonsai from cliff on sea, north side Okinawa."

"Where is the tree now?" Daniel asked, surprised that he hadn't heard of this before.

Mr. Miyagi turned off the trail they'd been following to take a shortcut to the palisade. Daniel stood next to him and gazed out onto the magnificent Pacific.

"Natural bonsai there, in Devil's Cauldron," Mr. Miyagi said, pointing. The rocky cliffs formed a natural cove that looked like a deep pot or cauldron with the ocean bubbling at the bottom where the whitecaps broke on the boulders.

Daniel looked carefully but he could see no sign of the bonsai. All he saw was an inhospitable wall of rock.

"Time to practice, Daniel-san," Mr. Miyagi said, returning to the campsite a hundred feet away.

"Devil's Cauldron is a lovely place," Daniel said, recalling its beauty.

"It is, if you are bonsai. Very lovely, very safe," Mr. Miyagi said.

"Safe from what?"

"People," Mr. Miyagi said simply. "Now, ready. Time to begin *kata*."

Daniel stowed the collection case in the shade of an evergreen and prepared to begin his karate training in earnest. A *kata* was the most basic method of practicing and studying karate stances and techniques. A *kata* is a series of prearranged movements, including punches, kicks, parries, and blocks, done by one person as if he or she were actually in a fight. It required the student to perfect every aspect of the techniques, including not only power, but balance and breath.

Daniel stood in front of Mr. Miyagi and began what he knew would be the difficult and arduous task of learning a *kata*. He had no doubt it would be worth the trouble because Mr. Miyagi was always right about two things: karate and bonsai.

"Right hand up. Left hand up. Breathe in. Right hand down. Left hand down. Make fist. Breathe out. . . ."

Later, as they relaxed by the camp fire, Daniel returned to their earlier subject. Something about Mr. Miyagi's story of the natural bonsai nagged at him.

"Mr. Miyagi, why did you put your tree in that place?"

"When Miyagi go fight in World War II, no one to take care of tree if something happen to me. Figure best place put tree back where tree take care of self."

"There are a lot of places in nature easier to get to," Daniel said.

"Daniel-san, know how much collector pay for original bonsai? Thousands of dollars. Better tree live where no one can see."

"But you can't see it, either," Daniel said.

"Here I can see," Mr. Miyagi said, tapping his head. "And here I can see." He tapped his heart.

Sometimes it seemed it would be impossible to understand everything about Mr. Miyagi. "You're really something else," Daniel remarked.

●

Chapter 7

Two days later, Daniel and Mr. Miyagi were back in Reseda and getting ready for the finishing touches at "Mr. Miyagi's Little Trees."

Early in the morning, before leaving for the shop, Daniel collected the mail from the old tin box at the end of Mr. Miyagi's driveway. He quickly shuffled through the envelopes, hoping for a note from his mother. There was a postcard, and it assured him the doctors said Uncle Louie was doing fine and so was she. There was something else in the mail, too. It was from the All-Valley Championship Committee and it was addressed to Mr. Miyagi at the Miyagi-do *dojo*. It had to be the application for Daniel to return this year and defend his title. Daniel could feel his pulse quicken. The memory of his championship bout was very special. He could almost hear the roar of the crowd and feel the wave of excitement. Daniel was sure there was nothing in the world like the thrill of victory. He had to show this to Mr. Miyagi right away.

He found Mr. Miyagi in his garden shed, completely surrounded by the saplings they had collected in the woods, all of which still looked like saplings, not bonsai. One of the saplings was directly in front of Mr. Miyagi. Daniel approached silently and watched.

Mr. Miyagi studied the sapling with his eyes. Then he closed his eyes in motionless meditation. He opened his eyes again to study some more. He obviously wasn't yet satisfied.

"Haven't seen the right tree inside yet?" Daniel asked.

"When looking for what inside, not matter how long it take. Only matter what find inside," Mr. Miyagi said solemnly.

Daniel held up the envelope. "Well, I bet I know what's inside this," he said. "I bet it's an application for this year's All-Valley Tournament." He handed the envelope to Mr. Miyagi. Mr. Miyagi set it aside and resumed his study of the sapling.

"Aren't you going to open it?" Daniel asked.

Still looking at the tree, Mr. Miyagi spoke. "A mountain only has to be climbed one time, Daniel-san."

"But what if you like the view from the top?" Daniel asked, recalling the wonderful feelings winning had given him.

"Then better you look at view alone," Mr. Miyagi said. "Come, we go work." Methodically he put the sapling back on the shelf, turned out the lights, and led the way to the truck. Daniel picked the envelope up off the workbench and followed after his teacher.

"I know you don't believe in fighting, Mr. Miyagi,

but this isn't exactly fighting," Daniel said, trying to revive interest.

"Isn't exactly ballroom dancing," Mr. Miyagi said.

"Well, what if I decide to fill the application out myself?" Daniel asked, catching up to Mr. Miyagi by the door of his truck. Mr. Miyagi took a pen out of his pocket, uncapped it, and handed it to Daniel. Then he climbed up into the cab of his pickup truck and drove off, leaving Daniel with an application in one hand, a pen in the other, and considerable confusion in between.

He returned to the house, deciding to look at the tournament material before meeting Mr. Miyagi at the shop. He liked everything he saw. The more he looked at the brochure and the application, the more convinced he became that he just had to get Mr. Miyagi to change his mind.

Daniel grabbed the keys to his car, but then he had an idea for Mr. Miyagi.

Fifteen minutes later, he entered the shop where Mr. Miyagi was already at work, sanding a display case.

"Look what I brought," Daniel said, holding up the sapling Mr. Miyagi had been struggling with earlier. "I thought a change of scenery might help get what's inside to be outside."

"Very thoughtful of you, Daniel-san," Mr. Miyagi said.

"I knew you'd like it. Where should I put it?"

Mr. Miyagi cleared a work space for the tree.

Daniel placed it on the table. "There you go. All set."

Mr. Miyagi bowed thanks to Daniel and began looking at the sapling in its new light.

"Uh, I hope you don't mind," Daniel began nervously. "I opened the letter from the tournament. There was a note with the application. Would you like to hear what it says?"

"Sure," Mr. Miyagi said absently. He appeared to be paying a lot more attention to the tree than to Daniel, but Daniel knew he always heard everything.

Daniel opened the letter and read, " 'Under the new rules, the defending champion will only fight in the final match.' See, Mr. Miyagi, it cuts down the fights to just one. That's better than what I had to put up with last year, isn't it?"

"*Hai.*"

"And, let's face it. It's another year. I'm a lot more experienced. Right?"

"*Hai.*"

"So I should seriously reconsider all this and sign up. Right?"

"Wrong. Should seriously consider getting new pots for bonsai." Mr. Miyagi pointed to the pottery shop across the street. Daniel had to admit that Mr. Miyagi certainly knew how to close a discussion, but he wasn't quite ready to give up yet.

"You know, I don't see what the big deal is," Daniel said.

"Daniel-san," Mr. Miyagi said patiently. "Karate

used to defend honor. Defend life. Mean something. Karate used to defend plastic and metal trophy, it mean nothing. Now you find good pots."

Daniel felt like he'd been dismissed, for Mr. Miyagi sat down in front of the sapling, studied it for a few seconds, and then pulled out a piece of paper and began sketching quickly with a pencil. What had been inside was coming outside.

There was no point in Daniel's going on about the tournament. Mr. Miyagi's mind was completely made up — for now. Daniel decided to try again later. Now he would go over to the pottery store to see if they had any pots suitable for "Mr. Miyagi's Little Trees."

Chapter 8

All it took was one look, and Daniel knew that the girl in the pottery shop was special.

She was working on the pottery wheel when he entered the shop. She was concentrating so hard that she didn't even hear him come in. He watched in rapt fascination while she molded and guided the clay on the fast-turning wheel. At first, it was just a lump; then, under her careful guidance, the clay seemed to rise up from the wheel. She hollowed it with one hand while holding it securely on the outside with the other. A bowl seemed to just grow from the wheel. When the bowl had reached its full height, she began to make careful designs on the outside with a small pencil-like tool, turning the wheel much more slowly.

Daniel cleared his throat to announce his presence.

"Hi," the girl said. "I'm almost finished."

"That's okay. Take your time. It's fun watching."

"Thanks," she said and continued her task. Daniel thought she was about his age. She had rich-colored red hair and intense green eyes. Her skin was fair with a generous smattering of freckles. Daniel couldn't decide whether it was more fun to look at her or to watch her work.

The wheel stopped spinning. The girl examined her bowl critically. Satisfied with what she saw, she looked up at Daniel for the first time.

"Thanks for waiting. What can I do for you?" she asked.

"I was looking for some planters," Daniel said, glancing around the work area while the girl carefully lifted her bowl off the wheel and carried it over to the kiln. Daniel saw a lot of pots, planters, and bowls around the work area, all in various stages of completion. He also saw, tacked to the wall, one half of a picture. The half that was there showed the red-headed girl rappeling down the face of a mountain. She was wearing shorts and hiking boots and looked remarkably happy, considering how high up the mountain she was.

"What size planter?" the girl asked.

"Oh, I don't know," Daniel said. "Like this, I guess." He held his hands in an oval shape, about nine inches long. "For bonsai trees. I'm from the shop across the street."

"Oh, right. I noticed there was some cleaning up going on over there. Welcome to the neighborhood."

She shut the kiln, wiped her clay-covered hands on her apron, and offered to shake with Daniel. "I love bonsai," she continued. "They're so perfect."

"You should come over and take a look when we move our trees in. And you can meet my partner."

"I haven't even met *you* yet," she reminded him.

"Oh, Daniel LaRusso," he said.

She smiled. "Jessica Andrews," she said.

"Is that you?" he asked, pointing to the torn photograph.

"Yup. I was climbing the mountain to get different clays for the pots. Like to come along sometime?"

The thought of relying on a rope, even a thick one, for his life made Daniel feel a little sick. The thought of spending time with Jessica made him feel a lot better. "Yeah, sure," he lied eagerly. "What happened to the other half of the picture?"

"Elizabeth Anne Rooney," Jessica said with more than a little spite in her voice.

Before Daniel could inquire further into that, there was a knock on the door and a delivery man announced he had three large cartons. She told him to bring the truck around to the rear. Then she turned to Daniel. "So, what should we do about your planters?" she asked.

"Well, I had this idea for planters with a little bonsai on the side — sort of like our trademark."

Jessica smiled. She obviously liked the idea. "Why don't I make one up and if, you know, everything's okay with the design and price, we'll go from there, okay?"

"Sounds okay to me," Daniel said.

"I've got to go," Jessica said, hearing the delivery man at the rear door.

"Well, see you soon," Daniel said, but he didn't really want to leave right then.

"How soon?" Jessica asked.

Daniel couldn't believe his luck. "Well, are you busy tonight?"

"No."

"Then I'll see you tonight — I mean, if you want to."

"About seven?"

"Seven it is," Daniel said.

"I live upstairs. Just knock. 'Bye."

She pivoted on her toes and headed for the rear door. Daniel watched her go. Her fluid motion left him almost breathless. Thoughts of the evening to come left him elated. It was another thirty seconds before he could turn and walk out of the store himself. He checked his watch to see how long it would be until he returned. Six hours and forty-three minutes.

When he returned to the bonsai shop, he found Mr. Miyagi hard at work on the bonsai. He'd finished his drawing and had it up in front of him. He clipped away at the sapling, and under his careful guidance it was being transformed into the bonsai in the picture. Daniel thought it magical the way Mr. Miyagi could make a bonsai from a sapling.

"You found it," Daniel said in wonder.

"Thanks to you," Mr. Miyagi said.

"I didn't do anything. Hey, it looks great."

"You find anything?" Mr. Miyagi asked him.

"Yeah, a date," Daniel answered, laughing. "You didn't send me over there just to look at pots, did you?"

Miyagi smiled and Daniel knew it had been a setup.

"I knew it. I could see your fine hand. And, speaking of fine hands, what should I do about this?" he asked, pulling the tournament application out of his pants pocket.

"Don't look at Miyagi for answer, Daniel-san. Like bonsai live inside tree, answer live inside you."

"Inside me right now's just a lot of confusion. I mean, I could put a pen to this and end up champion again."

"Or put match to it and let confusion go up in smoke."

Daniel looked inside himself. He knew he wasn't ready to learn the answer yet. He didn't like Mr. Miyagi's solution, but he wasn't happy with the idea of proceeding against his friend's will. He sighed to himself. The safe answer was to put off a decision for now.

He looked over Mr. Miyagi's shoulder some more while the old man finished trimming the sapling. He looked at the sketch and he had an idea. It was something he was pretty sure Mr. Miyagi would agree with, but he wanted to surprise him.

"Can I borrow that?" he asked, pointing to the sketch.

Mr. Miyagi removed the sketch from the wall and handed it to Daniel. "Yours to keep," he said.

That was just what Daniel needed. He had a good use for the six hours and forty-three — now thirty-six — minutes until seven o'clock.

Chapter 9

Daniel walked up the steps to Mr. Miyagi's house two at a time.

"Hey, Mr. Miyagi!" he called eagerly. There was no answer, but Daniel knew he was home because his truck was parked in the front. It was about six o'clock. He had an hour to change and drive back into town to pick up Jessica, but first, he had something to show his partner.

Daniel entered the house and checked out the living room. There was no sign of Mr. Miyagi. He passed through the house and into the yard. There at the back, in the toolshed, he found Mr. Miyagi packing up some of his own tools to take into the shop.

"Hi," Daniel said. "Look what I got." Proudly Daniel showed Mr. Miyagi the flyer he was having printed. It showed a picture of a bonsai — the one Mr. Miyagi had drawn that morning — and gave the name and address of the store and the services and goods they provided.

Mr. Miyagi looked at it carefully. "Daniel-san,

very nice, but we don't have this in the budget."

"It's in the revised budget," Daniel said. Then to assuage the doubt that crossed Mr. Miyagi's face, he continued. "Look, it's going to be great. It'll put us on the map."

"No more talk," Mr. Miyagi said. "Don't you have date tonight?"

Daniel smiled. "Yeah, and I've got to change. Can I borrow one of your fancy shirts for tonight?"

Mr. Miyagi nodded. "Wear one with the big orchids. Women no can resist big orchids."

"Sounds like the voice of experience," Daniel teased.

"Used to be voice. Now just a whisper."

Daniel helped Mr. Miyagi carry the tools to his truck. There was something about working with Mr. Miyagi that he always thoroughly enjoyed. They worked like real partners, understanding one another, knowing almost instinctively how to work together. This was as true of karate study as it was of carrying things to the truck. Daniel realized that it was impossible for him to even consider training for the tournament without Mr. Miyagi. Nor would he want to. His mind was then made up as surely as Mr. Miyagi's had been from the beginning.

When they were done loading the toolboxes, they returned to Mr. Miyagi's living room where Mr. Miyagi had some personal things he wanted to take to the shop. Daniel paused in front of the fireplace. It seemed as good a time as any to share his decision with Mr. Miyagi.

"Here's one tournament application that won't

see the light of day," Daniel said, pulling the crumpled paper from his pocket a final time. He struck a match, lit the application, and tossed it into the fireplace.

"Good, Daniel-san. Save on Band-Aids."

"You kidding? They never landed a hand on me last year," Daniel said defensively.

"Couple of feet. Elbow. Knee, maybe."

The two exchanged glances and laughed. The fact was that Daniel had taken quite a beating in order to win last year. He wouldn't miss the bruises at all.

Chapter 10

"Well, hello!" Daniel said, his face lighting up when Jessica came to the door.

"Hi. Nice shirt," she said.

"Thanks." Daniel smiled to himself. Mr. Miyagi would be pleased with the compliment. "So, what would you like to do?"

They walked toward Daniel's car as Jessica spoke. "Well, I have something to tell you first, which might make you not want to have anything to do with me."

"Why? What have you got? Measles, chicken pox?" Daniel teased. He couldn't imagine anything that would make him not want to be with Jessica.

"No. I've got a boyfriend. He was in the ripped half of the picture. I ripped it two months ago when we broke up."

"Because of Elizabeth Anne Rooney?" Daniel said, recalling her remark about what had happened to the other half.

"Yeah." Jessica sat down on a bench at a bus stop near Daniel's car, overlooking the street and the bonsai shop. "We were both a little dumb about it. But we've been talking on the phone, and we're going to give it another try when I go home."

"Where's home?" Daniel sat down next to her.

"Columbus, Ohio. I'm going back after Thanksgiving. So, that's it. I didn't want to lead you on or anything. I know I came on kind of strong in the shop this morning. I hope you don't mind."

"No, it was, uh" — Daniel searched for the word — "refreshing," although this conversation wasn't refreshing at all. It was disappointing.

"Well, I've been here two months and I haven't made any friends."

Daniel could hardly believe that. How could somebody so pretty and so nice go friendless for two months?

"Well, you just made your first friend," Daniel said, offering his hand. They shook, in friendship. Then Daniel began thinking out loud. "Boy, wait until Mr. Miyagi hears about this." Mr. Miyagi might have been right about the orchid shirt, but he'd been wrong about the girlfriend. Nevertheless, Daniel was prepared to be Jessica's friend as long as she'd have him and certainly up until the day she actually got on the plane for Columbus.

"Who is Mr. Miyagi?" Jessica asked.

"He's my partner. Hey, how would you like to meet him?" Daniel stood up from the bench. Jessica followed. "You are about to meet the greatest guy," he said enthusiastically. "He's smart. He's funny. You got a problem; he's got an answer. He's like no one you've ever met. And he's my best friend."

They crossed the street together and met Mr. Miyagi coming out of the shop. Daniel waved a greeting.

"Hey, Mr. Miyagi," he called, and when they reached the doorway, Daniel made the formal introductions. "This is Jessica Andrews from Columbus, Ohio, and across the street." He pointed to the pottery shop. "And Jessica, this is Mr. Miyagi from Okinawa and Reseda."

Mr. Miyagi bowed to Jessica. She bowed in return. Daniel had noticed, being with Mr. Miyagi, that a lot of people were uncomfortable bowing. Jessica seemed to feel right at home. As far as Daniel was concerned, that was three points in her favor.

"Welcome to the neighborhood," Jessica said graciously. "How's it going so far?"

"Never knew retirement would be such hard work," Mr. Miyagi said. Then he turned to Daniel and handed him the keys to the shop. "Make sure lock up when you leave." Then he bowed his farewell to Daniel and Jessica and headed for his truck.

"Where'd you meet him?" Jessica asked Daniel, following him into the darkened shop.

Daniel switched on the lights. "He used to work where I used to live. And a couple of things happened and he started to teach me karate, and we became friends."

"He sure doesn't look like the karate-teacher type," Jessica said.

Daniel was amused. She was right. Most people thought karate teachers looked the way the Cobra

Kai teacher, John Kreese, did. They were supposed to have beady eyes, fierce looks, and incredibly strong torsos. They were also supposed to wear *gi*s all the time and brandish their black belts. They definitely weren't supposed to look like benevolent Buddhas, the way Mr. Miyagi did.

"He doesn't act like it much, either," Daniel told Jessica as they walked around the shop. "Half the time he teaches me stuff, and I don't even know what's being taught. There are karate lessons everywhere, you know."

"What do you mean?"

"I'll show you," Daniel said. "Come sit down." He pulled up two fruit cartons and they sat facing one another. "Now, remember what you were doing with your hands when I watched you make that bowl this morning?"

Jessica looked at Daniel skeptically, but he told her to mimic the motions. She began moving her hands as if she were using them to form a bowl on her potter's wheel.

"Okay, now raise it a bit, like the bowl is getting taller."

Leaving her left hand low, as if to hold the base, Jessica raised her right hand, guiding the smooth wet clay at the rim of the bowl. Daniel nodded.

"Now, say I'm going to grab you," he said, reaching for her right hand. "Then up!"

She followed his instructions, hooking her arms through his, and catching him just above the elbow. She really had him trapped.

"Okay, now raise your knee and pull in."

As she did so, she yanked him forward, pulling his head toward her knee. It was easy to see that if they were actually in combat, she'd have Daniel trapped and looking for the Band-Aids — once her knee connected with his nose.

They were so involved in the karate exercise that they didn't hear the door open.

"Room for one more down there?" someone asked snidely.

Daniel looked up and was surprised to see two men there. The one who had spoken looked like a thug. He seemed to be accustomed to making smart remarks and getting away with it.

"We're not open," Daniel said quickly, disengaging himself from Jessica's hold.

"Door was," the thug said.

"I meant, for business."

"We came for a different kind of business," the man said. Daniel didn't like the tone of his voice at all. He felt a chill.

Then, for the first time, he noticed the other man. He was younger — no older than Daniel — but there was something about him that set off an alarm in Daniel's memory. Daniel knew he'd never seen him before, but he had a look that was very familiar, and menacing. He had the look of John Kreese.

"Hi," the younger man said to Jessica. Jessica returned the greeting coolly.

"Well, we were just leaving," Daniel said, trying to shepherd the duo out of the shop before they started any trouble. "So, if you'll tell me what you want. . . ."

The thug turned to Daniel and came to the point. "We heard you're not entering the All-Valley this year. Is it true?"

"Where'd you hear that?" Daniel asked, surprised. As far as he knew, the only people who knew that were himself and Mr. Miyagi.

"Is it true?"

"Yes, it's true," Daniel told him.

"Well, we'd like you to reconsider."

Daniel glanced at the younger man. "Is that why you're here?" he asked.

"Right. I need your title."

"So, enter the tournament and go for it," Daniel said.

The younger man glared at Daniel. "Maybe you didn't hear me," he said. "I need *your* title. Look, let me put it another way. You don't enter; it affects my financial future. And I'm not going to let that happen."

"I don't think you have a choice," Daniel said, wondering what the guy was talking about. Was someone paying this man to beat Daniel in the tournament?

"Yes, I do. *You* don't. Where's that application?" the younger man asked the thug. The older man removed an application from his pocket and handed it to him.

"Sign it," the guy said, pushing it into Daniel's face.

"No."

The young man lunged at Daniel, but his friend restrained him. "Let him sleep on it," he said.

"Right, sleep on it," the challenger said. Then he turned to Jessica. "Nice meeting you," he said politely.

"Slimeball," Jessica responded.

When they were gone, Daniel apologized to Jessica for the unpleasant encounter and told her about the championship. He tore up the application. He wanted to forget the incident, at least for the rest of his evening with Jessica. They turned out the lights and locked the door to the shop.

Daniel could feel the pieces of the torn-up application in his pocket. It made him think. The two strangers were gone, but Daniel had a bad feeling that he hadn't seen the last of them.

Chapter 11

It was a beautiful morning. The bright California sun gleamed through the trees and into Mr. Miyagi's garden. But that wasn't what made it beautiful. What made it beautiful was that Daniel felt good. He'd had a great time with Jessica the night before, in spite of knowing about her boyfriend. He also felt a tremendous sense of relief since he'd made the decision about the tournament. He knew it was the right decision, too. And, finally, he was about to work on his karate with Mr. Miyagi. Slowly but surely, Mr. Miyagi was teaching him the moves of the *kata*. Daniel was really enjoying it.

He stepped out of the house and into the yard, continuing the conversation they'd had at breakfast.

"So I told him and his goon that I wasn't going to fight. I have nothing to prove. I think I got my point across."

"Proud of you, Daniel-san."

"Oh, and Jessica kept talking about the shirt. You're right about orchids. Irresistible!"

Mr. Miyagi nodded sagely. "Enough talk. Time now to train."

"Mr. Miyagi, does training ever stop?" Daniel asked. He eased himself into an open-legged stance, the first position for his *kata*.

"Never," his *sensei* told him. "Now pay attention, Daniel-san. Very important lesson. Karate made of two things. *Go* and *ju*. Hard and soft," he translated. "Everybody thinks power of karate means hard karate. Hard block, hard punch. Real power of karate come from learn to be soft and alternate techniques."

Daniel stood up and put his hands on his hips. "Then how come you didn't teach me soft at first?" he asked.

"Because first must experience hard before able understand soft. Follow me." Mr. Miyagi began the familiar opening moves of the *kata*. Daniel did as his *sensei* did. "Now, feet together so. Hand in front — "

"Excuse me, Mr. Miyagi?" a voice called from the gate to the garden. Daniel and Mr. Miyagi stopped their exercise and turned to see their visitor.

He was about forty years old. There was a sadness in his face and his bearing. He walked slowly and carefully, as if he were embarrassed to be there.

"My name is Terry Silver," he said, startling both Daniel and Mr. Miyagi. "My karate master is Kim Sang Jang of South Korea. John Kreese was our school's number one student. In fact, I had loaned him money to start his own school here in California.

Word reached us in Korea only two months ago about what happened in the tournament last year. My teacher sends his apologies for John Kreese's dishonorable actions." Silver bowed to Mr. Miyagi and then to Daniel.

"Accept apology," Mr. Miyagi said simply.

"I wanted to help John regain his balance," Silver said.

"I hope you will be successful," Mr. Miyagi wished him graciously.

"Unfortunately I will not be. I buried John last week."

"He's dead?" Daniel asked in surprise. "What happened?"

"His doctor told me it was cardiac arrest, but I knew John better than anyone. He saved my life in Vietnam. Karate was his life. After he lost his students, his heart broke. That's what he really died of. A man goes off to war . . . comes home . . . for five years, ten years, he's fine. Then, one day something happens. You have to have been there to know what I mean."

"Have been. Do know," Mr. Miyagi said simply. But Daniel knew that it wasn't as simple as that. Mr. Miyagi had fought in World War II and he'd won the Congressional Medal of Honor. There was nothing simple about the courage he'd shown.

"Four-forty-second?" Silver asked. Those were the Japanese-American troops that fought in the European Theater during World War II, while their Japanese-American wives and children suffered in internment camps.

"Hai," Mr. Miyagi said.

"More medals of honor came out of that regiment than all the others put together. I'll bet you've been there." Then he turned to Daniel. "Is this your student? The champion?" he asked.

"Yes," Daniel said.

Silver bowed to Daniel. "Our apologies to you, too. John had vowed to apologize himself. He was going to, but . . ."

Then Daniel thought he understood about the look of sadness in Terry Silver's manner. He was sad about the death of a friend, but his grief was for the friend whose soul had been lost a long time earlier in the jungles of Vietnam.

"I'm sorry for interrupting your training," Silver said. "I just wanted to finish John's work for him." He turned to leave.

"Mr. Silver," Mr. Miyagi said. Silver stopped and turned. "Very sorry to hear about death of friend."

"Yeah, me, too," Daniel added. He was touched by Silver's sorrow.

"He wasn't like that. The way you saw him, I mean. The man was a hero."

The word echoed in Daniel's mind long after Silver had left the garden.

Hero.

Chapter 12

Daniel could hardly believe the transformation of the fruit-packing warehouse to a bonsai shop, but it was happening, right before his eyes, and all because of the hard work of his hands and Mr. Miyagi's.

He straightened out his back, standing up from the difficult work of sanding a display case, and looked around him. The whole place smelled of fresh paint and new wood. The walls gleamed, the cases and shelves were almost ready for the plants. They'd be able to open within a week, and since Daniel had been peppering the neighborhood with their flyers, he was sure business would be good. There seemed to be so much to look forward to that the work went quickly and well.

"Hi," came an interruption from the door. Daniel looked up. It was Jessica, and that meant it was a welcome interruption. She was carrying a big canvas bag. "Eat yet?" she asked.

"No," he said, putting down his sanding block

and straightening up once again. He wiped his hands on his jeans and carried the heavy bag for her, putting it on the newly sanded counter.

Jessica removed a large bowl, covered with aluminum foil, and opened it. "See, I made too much macaroni and cheese," she explained.

"No way," Daniel said. "You can't make too much macaroni and cheese. It's my favorite."

"So you're an expert?" she asked, handing him a fork for a taste.

"When it comes to macaroni and cheese, I'm the last word in all north Jersey."

"Be honest," she said and waited patiently.

Daniel made a big show of carefully selecting a morsel, examining it, as if checking the color and texture. He'd seen people taste wine and he tried to look like they did. He sniffed the macaroni and nodded sagely. Then he put the morsel into his mouth and pretended to take a long time making up his mind.

"On a scale of one to ten . . . " he began.

"Yes?"

"Eleven!"

"Well, just for that, I have something for you," she said. She reached into the bottom of the canvas bag and pulled out a ceramic planter.

It was exactly what Daniel had wanted. It was oval-shaped, and a rich deep blue. On the side was a perfect replica of the Miyagi bonsai. Daniel was astonished.

"It's beautiful," he told her.

"Thank you," she said.

"No. The thanks go to *you* and, actually, I have something for you."

He reached into his shirt pocket and found the surprise he'd been keeping for Jessica. He handed her two tickets. She looked at them.

"The Downstairs," she read, pleasure in her voice.

"Yeah, it's this great club. Live music. I figured it would be a nice going-away present for you. It's the night before you leave."

"Hey, great!" Jessica said. "I didn't know you liked to dance."

"That's why God gave me feet!" Daniel said, grinning. Jessica was smiling, too. She had the nicest smile, warm and friendly and genuine. Daniel thought she was a very special person and decided her boyfriend had been a fool even to look at Elizabeth Anne Rooney. Maybe . . .

The door chime sounded abruptly, breaking the moment. Daniel saw with dismay that the two bullies who wanted him to enter the tournament were back.

"What stinks in here?" the younger man said.

"Yeah, smells like something died," the older thug said.

"Must be the smell of a yellow streak," the younger one said.

"All right now, get out," Daniel said. "We're closed."

The pair ignored Daniel. They sashayed through

the shop, handling tools and running their fingers along the new cabinets. They left long smears on the clean wood.

"What's this? A mix?" the young guy asked, sticking his finger in the macaroni and cheese and tasting it.

"Enough's enough," Daniel said. "Get out."

"Sign the application yet?" the challenger asked.

"Look, I told you, I'm not fighting — you or anyone else. Now take your friend and get out."

"Mistake number one, pal," he said. "You are fighting me. The name's Mike Barnes, soon to be followed by the word Champion."

On signal from Mike, the thug leaped toward the display case Daniel had been sanding, swung his arm in a huge arc, and chopped through three shelves with one karate swing. At the first crack, Daniel ran to him and tried to shove him away. The thug lunged at Daniel, but Daniel was ready. He bent one knee and pushed the other foot out low, as if he were using it to propel a shovel into the earth. It was an ankle-level kick and it did the job, unbalancing the thug and sending him tumbling to the floor.

He rolled away from Daniel quickly, rising as he reached the place where Jessica stood. Without a second's hesitation, she took her big, heavy casserole dish and shoved it at his stomach. He grunted and dropped to the floor.

Without any apparent thought, Mike spun toward Jessica and kicked her in the ribs. She doubled over and backed off behind a counter for protection.

Daniel attacked in earnest. He charged with a fierce punch. Mike blocked it.

"Good punch," Mike sneered. "But not good enough."

Mike was in the center of the room. Daniel circled him, waiting for the opportunity to charge. Mike was good, though. Really good.

Daniel threw a kick. Mike blocked, swatting Daniel's ankle like a mosquito. Daniel recovered easily.

"Not bad," the bully jeered.

Daniel continued to circle. Mike kept his arms moving, and hopped lightly on his feet, prepared to block anything Daniel could throw, waiting for his chance.

Daniel punched again. It got closer to the target, but Mike's parries were good.

"Getting better," Mike said, still teasing cruelly.

Daniel faked with his right hand, hoping to distract Mike enough to score with his left. Mike deflected both punches and grabbed Daniel by his shirt. He lifted him off the floor and tossed him easily through a Japanese *shoji* screen that separated the shop from the workroom. Before Daniel could stand up on his own, Mike grabbed his shirt again and pulled him up toward him.

"Why are you being so stubborn?" he demanded.

Daniel used the momentum of Mike's tug to begin his renewed attack. He punched Mike hard in the stomach. Mike barely flinched. He simply picked Daniel up again and threw him through another *shoji* screen, shattering the delicate wood and ripping the paper. This time, Mike didn't give Daniel an opportunity to counterattack. He pulled him up and in a single motion, threw him at one of the finished display cases. Daniel collapsed into the glass, shattering it as he went.

"I'm running out of patience, LaRusso. Now sign and let's get on with it." He thrust an application and a pen at Daniel. Daniel accepted the offering and then ripped the application in half.

Mike was about to begin his unusual persuasion technique again, when the shop's door opened. Mr. Miyagi entered. Mike picked up a big fruit crate and threw it directly at Mr. Miyagi, but the old man was too quick for that maneuver. He ducked, allowing the crate to crash through the shop's window. Mr. Miyagi didn't flinch.

"Nail him!" Mike commanded. His thug dived toward Mr. Miyagi. Mr. Miyagi blocked the flying kick with his left hand and countered with a lightning sweep that sent his assailant hurtling through the final *shoji* in the shop. Mr. Miyagi faced Mike, fire in his eyes.

"I'm not afraid of you, old man," Mike taunted.

"Mistake number one," Mr. Miyagi said, advancing toward Mike swiftly.

"*Kiaiiii!*" Mike's explosive attack began. He charged and punched.

Mr. Miyagi deflected the punch with one hand and grabbed Mike's wrist with the other. "Mistake number two," he said calmly.

Mike tried to wrench his wrist from Mr. Miyagi's grasp, but Mr. Miyagi held tightly. Furiously Mike swung at Mr. Miyagi with his free hand, but his motion was hampered by Mr. Miyagi's hold. Apparently without effort, Mr. Miyagi seized his other wrist, now holding Mike by both hands.

"Mistake number three. You're out," Mr. Miyagi announced. With that, he shifted the weight in his hips, and swung around, pulling Mike up over his shoulder and jettisoning him toward the door. He flew out, end over end, like a tumbleweed in the wind.

The thug pulled himself up out of the mass of sticks and paper that had been a *shoji* and stumbled after Mike. He helped Mike up, and the two of them staggered to their car. When they were safely out of Mr. Miyagi's reach, the thug turned and delivered his final threat.

"Hey, Buddha-head, you can't watch the kid all the time!"

Then they were gone. But for how long?

Jessica helped Daniel and Mr. Miyagi clean up the wreckage in the shop. When they were done, the place looked little better than it had the day Daniel had rented it. Two-weeks worth of work was destroyed in five-minutes worth of fighting. It seemed to Daniel like a very bad trade-off.

When the cleanup was finished, Daniel walked Jessica back to her shop and then returned to drive home with Mr. Miyagi, who seemed extraordinarily cheerful under the circumstances. He sang off-key with a tape as he drove.

"How can you just sit there singing?" Daniel asked.

"Feel lucky," Mr. Miyagi said.

"Lucky that our whole shop just got annihilated?"

"Lucky that bonsai did not. We can rebuild the shop, Daniel-san. We can't rebuild the trees. We will sell a few of trees we have now, use money to buy some new *shoji*, and start shelves and cabinets all over again."

"And what if they come back?" Daniel asked, looking on the dark side.

"One thing at a time, Daniel-san."

"And I bet you thought retirement was going to be dull," Daniel teased.

"With you around, Daniel-san, things are never dull."

Mr. Miyagi turned the truck into his driveway. Daniel's heart fell when the truck's headlights swept Mr. Miyagi's front porch, for where there should have been dozens of bonsai trees, there were none. The racks were there, unharmed, but all the trees were gone. In their stead was a familiar piece of paper, tacked to the wood of the racks. Daniel didn't have to look at it to know what it said. It was an application for the All-Valley Championship Tournament.

Chapter 13

"How much further?" Jessica asked two days later as she followed Daniel through the woods to the cliffs by the ocean. They each wore heavy-duty hiking clothes and carried thick ropes, clips, hammers, and spikes — everything they would need for rappeling on the palisade.

"It should be right up ahead," Daniel said, trying to recall the exact location.

"What if it's not there?"

"It's there," Daniel said. It *had* to be there.

"I don't know," Jessica said. "If something were worth that much money, people would look for it, don't you think?"

"If they knew where to look," Daniel said.

They walked on in silence. Since Mike and his thug had ruined the shop and stolen the bonsai, Daniel had been concentrating on ways to repair the damage. He'd reported the theft to the police, but he had little faith that any good would come of that. That brought the whole issue down to money. Money to buy new *shoji*, money to buy more wood for cabinets, and, most of all, money to buy new bonsai. All of his funds were gone. There was only one other source of money Daniel could think of: Mr. Miyagi's natural bonsai.

If it was worth half of what Mr. Miyagi said, then they could sell it and have money to spare. They'd be in business in no time.

They sat at the campsite Daniel and Mr. Miyagi had used on their collecting expedition and Jessica prepared the ropes and other equipment while they talked.

"I still think you should have asked Mr. Miyagi before going after his tree," Jessica said.

"Look, we don't sell the tree, he loses his business. Without the business, he has no income. I mean, his Social Security won't even cover the expenses on his rowboat. Don't you see? The tree's like money in the bank."

"Great," Jessica said without enthusiasm. "So now we're robbing a bank."

She stood up, and handed Daniel his rope. They were ready to proceed. Daniel led her along the last section of the trail to the palisade, and then they followed along the edge until they came to Devil's Cauldron. Jessica had never seen it and it was Daniel's first close-up look. It was immense, frightening, and beautiful.

"You know where we are?" Jessica asked. "This is the rim of an extinct volcano. Look, it connects with the ocean."

Daniel leaned over the rim and looked to the bottom of the Cauldron, where the waves broke on the craggy volcanic rocks. It was a long way down.

He took out the binoculars and scanned the walls of the Cauldron.

"How are you going to find one little tree in all of this?" Jessica asked.

"Knowing Mr. Miyagi, he probably put it in the hardest place to get to." He was silent for awhile while he examined the rocky face. Then he saw it. About two thirds of the way down there was a ledge, and beneath the ledge, there was a small indentation in the rock. Somehow, plants had managed to grow in the meager soil there, clinging onto life and the cliff at the same time. It was the most inaccessible place in the entire Cauldron. That was the place Mr. Miyagi would have chosen.

He handed the binoculars to Jessica and pointed.

"Oh, boy," she said. "He really knows how to pick them!"

Daniel wasn't certain whether rappeling was more fun or frightening. It certainly was the latter. He was suspended from the top of Devil's Cauldron by a rope — a good strong rope. He controlled his descent by feeding rope upwards. He could drop quickly and he could drop slowly. He decided to drop slowly to avoid dropping *very* quickly.

"Don't worry. You're doing okay," Jessica assured him from above as she finished her own preparations and began her descent.

Daniel let out some more rope and used his feet to push away from the cliff so that the craggy rocks wouldn't rip at him. "Boy, Mr. Miyagi must have been like Spiderman to get down to this."

"What if he tells you to put it back?" Jessica asked.

"You don't understand. That shop is his dream. When he sees what we've got for him, it's going to be like Christmas and New Year's all wrapped up into one."

"I hope it's not more like April Fool's," Jessica said heavily.

Daniel stopped his descent and clipped his rope the way Jessica had shown him. He swung gently until he had a footing at the indentation where he thought the tree was — and it *was* there. Jessica lowered herself the rest of the way and maneuvered her rope until she was standing in the indentation next to Daniel.

"It's been here for almost fifty years," Daniel said, gazing at the natural bonsai, still no more than ten inches tall. Its miniature limbs and needles told a story of survival under the roughest of circumstances. For nearly fifty years, it had stood firm against the elements, taken the battering of rainstorms and winds. For fifty years, its roots had held their rocky ground against the intrusion of weeds fighting the same battle. For fifty years, its only enemy had been nature.

Daniel took a trowel from his belt and began digging carefully at the base of the tree. He knew he had to protect the plant's roots.

"Nice and easy," he spoke to the tree. "I won't hurt you. From now on, regular haircuts, gourmet plant food. No more wind. No more cold."

He eased the plant out of the sandy earth, where its roots had survived for so long. He was about to slip it into a collection bag when the clip that held his rope slid a notch, shifting him downward a few inches. The movement terrified Daniel. Frantic, he grabbed at the rope and held on for his life. The rope held fast, but the bonsai did not. Daniel had let go of it when he grasped the rope and it tumbled pathetically down the face of the cliff, bouncing off the rocks and, finally, into a tidal pool.

"The salt water will kill it!" Daniel howled.

"Okay, don't panic," Jessica said, trying to sound calm. "Go very slowly. One step at a time. Follow me."

Patiently she led him down the rest of the face of the cliff, as far as their ropes would go. But when they reached the end of their ropes, they were still three feet above the bottom of Devil's Cauldron.

"Unhook," Jessica said, releasing the hooks that held her to her ropes. Smoothly she lowered herself to the rocky surface below. Daniel did the same. He ran over to the tidal pool and retrieved their precious quarry. Jessica offered him her canteen. He poured fresh water on the roots, rinsing salt off as best he could.

"Is it going to be okay?" she asked.

"I don't know. We have to wash the roots and then get some moss around them." Then he spoke to the tree again. "You okay, old fellow? We've got to get you out of here and get you home fast." Carefully he surrounded the roots with fresh moss and wrapped the new root ball in protective plastic. He secured the tree in his backpack. "Let's go," he said.

They turned to reattach themselves to the ropes and begin the long ascent to the top of Devil's Cauldron when they saw, in horror, that the ropes were already going up. Without them!

"Hey!" Daniel shouted, grabbing for the rope, but it was too late. Then, as the ropes swept upwards toward the top, something came down in their place. It was a piece of paper. And a pen.

Daniel knew just what it was, and it wasn't good news.

Chapter 14

"Hey, LaRusso! How you doing?" Mike Barnes's voice boomed down into Devil's Cauldron, echoing off the rocks.

"This isn't a joke anymore," Daniel said.

"It never was."

"So let our ropes down!"

"Sure, but first you've got to sign the application."

"Forget it!" Daniel yelled back.

"Okay, all right. I'll forget it. And you can forget it, too, when the tide comes in about twelve feet. Hope you brought a raft!"

Daniel could hear his very unpleasant laugh. He turned to Jessica. "What are our chances of getting out of here without a rope?" he asked.

"None," she said simply.

Daniel made up his mind quickly. He picked up the application and signed it. "Now get us out of here!" he yelled.

The ropes came tumbling down the cliff. Before Mike and his goon had a chance to change their minds, Daniel and Jessica hooked themselves back onto the rigs.

"I'm such a jerk," Daniel said, speaking to himself as much as to Jessica. "I signed it."

"You couldn't know this was going to happen," Jessica said.

She was right, but it was little comfort. They began their ascent. "Hey, Barnes!" he yelled. "You want this so bad, work for it!" he said, waving the application. "Pull us up!"

Mike's face appeared over the top of the cliff. He laughed at Daniel's suggestion, but in a moment, they started upward.

"Just because you signed it doesn't mean you have to go through with it," Jessica reminded Daniel.

He shook his head. "I don't work that way. Sometimes I wish I did, but I don't. Period. I've got to fight him."

They continued upward silently. Then, before they reached the top of the rim, they stopped.

"Hey, come on," Daniel complained.

Mike leaned over the top of the cliff. "You are one heavy wimp, Daniel." He stretched his right hand toward Daniel. "The application."

"When we're up there," Daniel said. He wasn't taking any more risks, especially on Jessica's behalf.

Suddenly Jessica's rope slackened. Within a second, she'd dropped about ten feet. She screamed. The rope stretched taut. She held on tightly, her face pale with fear.

Mike's hand reached out to Daniel again. Daniel

handed him the application willingly.

"And don't even think about backing out, because then I'll be really angry and this will seem like a happy memory compared to what we'll do to you — and her," he said, motioning to Jessica. His head disappeared back over the top of the cliff.

Then nothing happened. Daniel tugged frantically at the rope. "Hey!" he yelled.

"What, sweetheart?" Mike's thug asked.

"I gave you the application, so pull us up!"

The thug's face appeared above. "The rates just went up," he said. "Give me the tree."

"Daniel, don't," Jessica said.

But he had to. He couldn't risk her life. He couldn't risk his own. Nothing was worth it.

Carefully holding onto the rope with one hand, Daniel removed the damaged bonsai with the other and handed it up to the thug.

"What are you going to do with it?" Mike asked.

"Replant it," the thug said. "Down there!" He held the precious bonsai over the edge of the cliff.

"No, don't!" Daniel and Jessica cried out together.

"Enough," Mike said, taking the tree from the thug. He snapped off one of the branches as if it were a twig. The cracking sound cut through Daniel's heart like a knife. Mike dropped the damaged tree on the ground and he and his thug left, laughing together.

Cautiously Daniel and Jessica completed the ascent on their own. Jessica helped Daniel crest the rim of Devil's Cauldron, and then they helped each other remove the rigs that had held them to the ropes.

When he could no longer put it off, Daniel turned to where he knew the natural bonsai lay.

An hour earlier, in the harsh hands of nature, the tree had been thriving. Now in the care of men, the tree was lying on the ground, its roots bare of their nourishing soil and saturated with salt. Its primary branch was torn from the trunk, and the needles crushed from Mike Barnes's careless footstep.

The cruelties of nature were a piece of cake compared to the cruelties of humankind.

Chapter 15

"Mr. Miyagi?"

Daniel spoke tentatively as he entered the shop. He didn't want to tell his friend what he had done.

Mr. Miyagi looked up from the display case he was building. Daniel stepped forward hesitantly. He held up the damaged bonsai.

"I didn't mean for this to happen. I really didn't. I'm really sorry."

Mr. Miyagi took the tree from him and studied the damage. He took it back into the workshop area where he had gardening tools, pots, and soil.

"I figured we could sell it so we wouldn't have to close the shop. I didn't want it to be my fault that your dream didn't come true. I knew whoever bought it would be really good to it and take care of it, maybe even better than it could take care of itself." Daniel pulled himself up short. "That's nuts. What am I talking about? How could anybody take care of it better than how you left it?"

Without answering Daniel's questions, Mr. Miyagi placed the bonsai carefully into Jessica's pot.

He packed the damaged roots in fresh earth and covered the earth with protective moss. He added water for nourishment. Then he examined the broken branch. He took some gooey black stuff, painted the wound with it, and replaced the branch, being sure to fit it exactly as it had been.

"Is it going to be okay?" Daniel asked.

Mr. Miyagi spoke for the first time. "Depend. If root strong, tree survive."

There was a knock at the door. A delivery man entered. "Where do the bonsai trees go?" he asked.

"Leave outside," Mr. Miyagi said.

"Trees?" Daniel asked, astonished. He followed the delivery man as far as the door and saw him unload hundreds of baby bonsai.

"You bought these? How?"

"*Hai*. Sold truck." Mr. Miyagi walked outside to supervise the unloading.

Daniel followed him. "Why didn't you tell me that's what you were going to do?"

"When I woke up, you were gone," Mr. Miyagi said. "Don't worry. Everything will be okay."

Daniel liked the sound of the reassuring words, but he knew that the trouble wasn't over. He told Mr. Miyagi that he'd signed up for the tournament and when Mr. Miyagi asked him why, he said, "Because I'm not you. I tried to be, but it didn't work. The softer I was, the harder it got until I didn't have a choice. I had to make a decision on the spot and I made it."

"Understand that," Mr. Miyagi said.

"You do?"

"*Hai*, but I don't support it."

"Mr. Miyagi, I don't stand a chance against this guy unless you train me."

"Understand that, too."

"Then you will train me?" Daniel asked.

"Will always train you, Daniel-san. But not for tournament. Cannot."

Mr. Miyagi picked up a tray full of bonsai and returned to the shop.

Daniel knew that was the close of that subject with Mr. Miyagi, for good. He would have to train on his own and hope for the best, but he couldn't expect much without the old man's help.

The next morning, he met Jessica at her house and invited her to go jogging with him. It was hard going for Daniel. He'd gotten out of shape with just a few weeks off from his training. He stopped to rest, leaning forward and breathing hard.

"You can't keep stopping like this," Jessica told him. "You've got to build up your wind."

"Why? So there will be more of it to knock out of me?" He straightened up and they continued their workout, running side by side without talking.

A horn honked behind them. Terry Silver leaned out of a pickup truck and waved to Daniel. "Hi."

Daniel introduced him to Jessica.

"You training for the Olympics or something?"

"No, a karate tournament."

"The one you won last year? What's it called?"

"The All-Valley," Daniel told him.

"Good for you," Terry said. "A champion should

defend his title. John Kreese told me you had a lot of heart. Know how to front sweep?"

"Not really," Daniel said truthfully.

"Ask your Mr. Miyagi to show you. He'll know."

"I'm kind of training for this one myself," Daniel said.

Silver looked a little puzzled when he heard that, but he made no remarks. Instead he offered help. "I know a book on sweep techniques. I'll drop it off sometime. Best to Mr. Miyagi and nice to meet you, Jessica. Take care of our champion," he said before he drove off.

"That was a nice offer about the book," Jessica said.

"Yeah, it was," Daniel said. It was nice to have somebody offer to help him. It seemed to Daniel that lately everybody he'd been with, except Jessica and now Silver, was trying to get in his way. Even his best friend was trying to guarantee his failure. Terry Silver was a refreshing change. He started running again and promised himself he wouldn't stop to rest until the run was over.

Chapter 16

"Left and one! Right and two!" Daniel counted out karate punches as he jabbed at a heavy punching bag in Mr. Miyagi's backyard. Training was hard when he was working with a *sensei*. It was harder working without one. For one thing, he couldn't be sure he was doing the right thing. For another, he was lonely. Mr. Miyagi was at the shop, building shelves and installing the new *shoji*.

The gate to the garden slammed open. "Hey, you jerk! What did you call the cops for?" It was Mike Barnes and, as usual, he was angry.

Daniel turned and confronted him. "You don't belong here. Get out."

"What did you call the cops for?" Mike demanded.

"What did you steal the trees for?"

"You got no proof."

"Who left that application?" Daniel asked. "The tooth fairy?"

Mike fired a punch at Daniel that he was totally unprepared for. It sent him reeling backwards. Daniel recovered and counterattacked. Daniel was good, but Mike was better. He was sharper, with fancier techniques.

Daniel tried to give him everything. When he punched, Mike blocked. When he kicked, Mike dodged. In return, Mike landed powerful punches, seemingly at will, on Daniel. Daniel tried his winning kick from the All-Valley the year before — the crane technique. He rose on one foot and lifted his hands as if he were about to take flight, straight up. At just the right moment, he sprang up, kicking viciously at his opponent.

Mike grabbed the foot and held it by the ankle, dumping Daniel onto the ground unceremoniously. Then Mike stepped forward and put one of his feet on Daniel's throat, blocking his windpipe. Daniel struggled against Mike, but it wasn't working.

"How did you get into that tournament last year — much less win it? I'm on to you, buddy boy. There's no technique you've got that I can't counter. None."

Daniel had the awful feeling he was right. He had the worse feeling that unless Mike released him, he wouldn't even make it to the tournament.

Then another visitor arrived in Mr. Miyagi's garden. It was Terry Silver.

"Beat it, punk!" Silver ordered.

"Make me," Mike challenged him, releasing Daniel.

Terry Silver made short work of Mike. He blocked his punches and then defeated him with a sweep that sent him crashing to the deck.

"Now get up and get out."

Mike stumbled to his feet and practically ran to the gate. He was gone before Daniel stood up.

"You okay?" Silver asked.

Daniel rubbed at his throat and checked himself. "Yeah, thanks to you."

"Don't mention it," Silver said. "Look, I brought you the book." He handed it to Daniel. "And I also gave you an impromptu lesson on how effective sweeps can be."

"That was impressive," Daniel told him. "It really worked."

"That was a nasty character. Who is he?" Silver asked. Daniel explained the situation.

"He's going to be tough," Silver said. "Have you got someone to practice with?"

"No," Daniel told him.

"Well, let me show you something, then." He stood up and Daniel stood up next to him. Silver spent some time working with Daniel on sweeps. It was wonderful to have a teacher and a friend to work with. And Silver was a good teacher, too. Within fifteen minutes, Daniel felt secure with the sweep Silver had demonstrated. In fact, he was so secure that he was able to catch Silver off-guard and the man ended up on his rear.

"You okay?" Daniel asked, offering him a hand.

Silver smiled approvingly at him. "I'm fine, and so are you. Nice job. Look, everybody needs a teacher, Daniel. I'm opening up the Cobra Kai *dojo* again. Time to set things straight. Any time you want to train, I'm there for you. No strings attached. I mean that."

Daniel couldn't believe the generosity of the offer. "I appreciate that. And thanks for helping me out today, both with Mike Barnes and with the sweeps."

Solemnly Daniel bowed to Silver. Silver returned the bow and left.

When he'd gone, Daniel tried the sweep again, but it was hard to do alone. Daniel decided his workout for the day was over. It was time to go to the shop and see Mr. Miyagi. He had a hunch that he might be able to get some help from him after all. Quickly Daniel put away his equipment, showered, changed his clothes, and drove to the shop.

"Look, Daniel-san." Mr. Miyagi greeted him with a big smile. Jessica was standing next to him. "Beautiful, huh?" Mr. Miyagi held up some new planters Jessica had finished for them.

"I stayed up all night firing them," Jessica said.

"Yeah, they're great," Daniel said, but his mind was on something else. A thought had occurred to him. "Mr. Miyagi, do you know how to sweep?" he asked. He needed some work on the technique Silver had been teaching him. If only he could get Mr. Miyagi to open up.

"Of course," the man said.

"Would you mind showing me how?" Daniel asked.

"Couldn't have asked at a better time, Daniel-san," Mr. Miyagi said. He walked into the plant workroom and Daniel trailed him eagerly. Daniel could tell that Mr. Miyagi had been working with the new pots because there was soil all over the floor. It scrunched under their feet as they walked.

"I don't mean to get into anything complicated," Daniel said. "Just the basics would be great."

Mr. Miyagi walked back to the corner where they'd stowed their cleaning equipment. He took a broom and handed it to Daniel.

"Very easy. One hand up, one down. First left, then right."

Jessica laughed. That was more than Daniel could stand.

He glared at Mr. Miyagi. "It's no joke," he said angrily. "You don't want to show me, don't show me, okay? But don't make fun of me. Sorry for asking. It won't happen again. Ever."

Daniel handed the broom to Mr. Miyagi and then spun on his heel and left the shop, slamming the door behind him.

He'd show them.

Chapter 17

Daniel drove around in his car for hours. He needed to think, and the act of driving freed his mind for his thoughts. He drove in circles. He thought in circles.

Every time he went over recent events in his mind, he concluded that he had had no choice but to sign the paper and, having signed it, had no choice but to fight, and having decided to fight, had no choice but to train. If Mr. Miyagi trained him, he could win. If he trained himself, he'd lose. And if he was going to lose, why should he fight? He had to fight because he'd signed the paper. Begin again.

By nightfall, he'd made up his mind. He drove his car back into the center of Reseda and pulled up at the curb by the Cobra Kai *dojo*. He remembered the day, more than a year ago, when he'd looked through the window of the karate school, envious of its students. Now he would be one.

He looked through the window again. There he saw Terry Silver in a *gi*, performing a *kata*. He was magnificent. Daniel opened the door and entered.

"Hi," Daniel said. "That looked great."

Silver bowed politely. "Just trying to work the rust out. How are you doing?"

"Okay. Say, I gave your offer some thought and, uh, if it's not too much trouble, I'd like to take you up on it," Daniel said. "Well, you know, like on a short-term basis."

Silver's face lit up with joy. "Trouble? Are you kidding? It would be an honor to train with the champion. But how does Mr. Miyagi feel about it?"

Daniel shoved his hands in his pockets. Although he was certain he was doing the right thing, it did make him feel a little disloyal to his friend. "Mr. Miyagi doesn't really need to know about it," Daniel said.

"But he knows you're competing?"

"Yeah, he knows that. He just doesn't approve."

Daniel thought he saw a look flash across Silver's face. Disapproval? He wasn't sure. In an instant, it was gone. "Well, everyone has a right to his opinion, so I won't say anything. When would you like to start?"

"Whenever it's convenient for you."

"There's a *gi* hanging in the dressing room. I think it will fit you. How about now?"

Daniel had already made up his mind. Without hesitation, he strode to the dressing room.

Silver put Daniel to work right away.

"There are three things that make a champion — the three D's. Desire, devotion, and discipline. The first two, I can't teach. The last one, I can, but you have to be willing to receive it. Are you, Mr. LaRusso?"

"Yes," Daniel said.

"Yes, *sir*," Silver instructed him.

"Yes, sir," Daniel echoed.

"That's better. Now stand up straight." Daniel straightened to attention. "Over the years I've developed a system of intensive short-term training for situations just like this. It comes in two parts and has three rules. I call it Quick Silver. Rule number one: A man can't stand; he can't fight. Repeat it."

Daniel repeated the words.

"With conviction, Mr. LaRusso."

Daniel spat out the words. Silver nodded. Daniel felt a little bit like an inductee in the army, going through basic training. It wasn't what he was used to in karate, but he'd seen what Silver's methods could do, both in the brief skirmish Silver had had with Mike Barnes and with the impressive *kata* he'd executed while Daniel watched. Surely this man had something to teach Daniel. Daniel decided to accept his methods and learn his wisdom.

Silver led Daniel over to a metal frame in which he had clamped a two-foot length of two-by-four vertically, at ankle level.

"Sweep it," Silver instructed Daniel.

Trying to repeat the motions they'd worked on in Mr. Miyagi's garden earlier in the day, Daniel carefully picked up his right foot and meticulously moved it to the board, contacting the wood with the edge of his foot.

"Too low," Silver said.

"Any higher and I'll hit the knee," Daniel told him, aware of the real damage a knee-level sweep could cause.

Silver gave Daniel a hard look. "Mr. LaRusso, did you come here to teach, or to be taught?"

Daniel felt his stomach tighten. Silver wasn't at all like Mr. Miyagi, but he'd made his decision, and he was going to learn. He nodded and tried the movement again, this time hitting the board higher.

"We're not sweeping floors here," Silver said. "Put your hip into it. That's where the power is."

Daniel tried again, smacking against the board this time.

"Harder." He tried again, feeling the wood against the blade of his foot. "Harder!" He tried again.

"Ow!"

" 'Ow'? 'Ow' is not an acceptable *kiaii* in this *dojo*, Mr. LaRusso."

Daniel looked at his bare foot. It was swollen and reddening. It would be black and blue by morning.

"Isn't this a little bit extreme? Sir?"

"Kiaiiiii!" Silver swept the two-by-four with his foot and turned it into splinters. "Extreme situations require extreme measures, Mr. LaRusso. Come back in the morning. We'll start again. You did all right for the first day of training."

He bowed to Daniel and Daniel bowed in return. Then Silver disappeared into the office of the *dojo*. When he was gone from the room, Daniel sat on the floor and examined his foot. It hurt so much he could barely touch it.

Daniel drove home. He limped back into Mr. Miyagi's house, carrying his left shoe because it wouldn't fit on the swollen foot. He went around to his own room, avoiding Mr. Miyagi, who was in the backyard. He didn't want another confrontation or lesson in sweeping, with a broom, or anything.

He collapsed on his bed, exhausted, and stared at the ceiling, thinking about what tomorrow would bring at the Cobra Kai *dojo*, and whether he would ever have the endurance that Silver did.

There was a knock on his door. Mr. Miyagi came in, carrying a pail and a canister. Daniel slid his foot under a blanket.

"Saw you limping, Daniel-san. What happened to foot?"

"Oh, that foot," he said airily. "I must have banged it and didn't notice." The last thing he wanted was to have Mr. Miyagi hanging around and commenting on his training.

Mr. Miyagi put the pail on the floor and began pouring powder from the canister into it. "Soak foot in that. By tomorrow, you'll be fine."

Daniel wrinkled his nose at the foul odor of the powder. "Why? You have a new foot in there for me?" he asked.

"Have next best thing: new foot powder."

Daniel sniffed, then wrinkled his nose in disgust. "Smells like old foot powder. What's in there?"

"Better you don't know. Here." Gently he took

Daniel's foot and put it into the malodorous solution. Daniel could feel the healing power immediately.

"I don't know what I'd do without you," Daniel said gratefully.

"Probably spend a lot more time in doctor's office. Good night, Daniel-san."

Mr. Miyagi rose and left the room. Daniel was alone with the smelly foot powder and his memories of the evening spent at Cobra Kai. Although one event had led to the other, they were strangely conflicting. Daniel fell asleep thinking about that, his sore foot dangling in the water all night.

Chapter 18

Daniel was impressed with the results of Mr. Miyagi's magical powder. He was also relieved to be able to walk and work out the next day.

"Okay, what's the last thing Mr. Miyagi taught you?" Silver asked.

"*Kata*," Daniel said and began demonstrating the movements.

"*Kata*'s okay for working up a sweat, but it's not going to win you a tournament. Come over here and hold the bag." Daniel followed Silver to where a large and heavy leather-covered bag was suspended from the ceiling in a corner of the *dojo*. Daniel moved to the far side of the bag and held it as Silver had instructed.

"Rule number two: A man can't breathe; he can't fight." Silver paused to let the lesson sink in. "Now, imagine this is the enemy. These are his ribs right here." He pointed to the bag. "And behind his ribs, his lungs."

As if the word were a signal, Silver lashed out with a forearm strike, hitting the bag so hard that he almost knocked Daniel down. Daniel could barely believe the power.

"Now you try."

They switched places, Silver holding the bag, and Daniel set to strike the bag as Silver had done.

"No, no, wait," Silver said. "Let's do it over here." He led Daniel back to the metal rack. Only now, a fresh two-by-four had been placed at chest level. "Right there," Silver said, pointing to the target. "Lay into it."

Daniel did as he was told, and smashed his arm against the wood, wrenching his elbow terribly.

"Ow!" He rubbed his elbow and forearm. "Why do we have to do this?"

"Because you don't go hunting elephants with peashooters. And right now, Mr. LaRusso, a pea-shooter is about all you've got in your arsenal."

"I did okay with it last time," Daniel reminded the *sensei*.

"Wake up and smell the coffee, Mr. LaRusso." Silver reached over to the metal rack and spun the headpiece of the device around. On it was taped a photograph of none other than Mike Barnes. "Last time you weren't fighting this. The only thing standing between you and a very severe beating is what I'm teaching you. Now, do you want to get beaten because you're afraid of a little pain? Be my guest. But I don't want any part of it. I make wimps into winners. Not the other way around."

Silver retreated to his office, leaving Daniel alone with his thoughts. He looked at the picture of Mike.

He remembered the anger, the humiliation, the beating.

He breathed deeply, spun, and smacked the two-by-four with his sore arm. He did it again, and again, and as he worked, he didn't mind the pain or the swelling or the soreness. He concentrated on Mike Barnes's ribs and lungs.

Later, at home, he concentrated on some more smelly powder. He poured the ingredients into the bucket of warm water and immersed his damaged arm into the healing brew.

There was a knock at his door. He was so startled that he tipped the bucket. Its foul-smelling ingredients splashed all over the floor of his room. He had thought Mr. Miyagi was asleep. The last thing he needed was a lecture from the man who wouldn't lift a finger to help him.

"Can you come back later?" Daniel asked, but Mr. Miyagi had already entered. He regarded the scene, taking in the bruised elbow and the smelly mess on the floor.

"Daniel-san," he said kindly. "Why you do this to yourself?"

Daniel looked at him with steely eyes. " 'Because extreme situations require extreme measures,' " he recited.

Mr. Miyagi picked up a towel and helped Daniel mop up the mess. "That doesn't sound like you talking, Daniel-san."

Daniel took the towel from Mr. Miyagi and opened his door to invite the man to leave. "Well, it *is* me talking, and I'm sorry if you don't like it. But I've got problems and if you're not going to be part of the solution, don't give me a hard time about it. Okay?"

Daniel slammed the door after Mr. Miyagi. He poured some more powder into the bucket and immersed his arm. As with his foot, Daniel could feel the healing power of the mixture almost immediately, but he wondered how many times, how many beatings and bruises the mixture could heal. And could it heal a broken friendship?

Before he went to sleep, Daniel returned the powder to the cabinet in Mr. Miyagi's room. The old man slept soundly, snoring gently and peacefully. Moonbeams lit his room with a soft glow. Daniel tiptoed to the cabinet and then back to the door.

Before he left the room, his eyes lit on the natural bonsai on Mr. Miyagi's bedside table. It was just a skeleton. All of the needles had fallen off and the broken branch sagged away from the trunk. Daniel feared that even Mr. Miyagi's smelly healing potions would be useless against the damage he'd caused to the precious little tree.

Chapter 19

In the morning Daniel's arm felt better. A lot of things seemed to be going wrong, but the one thing that consistently worked for him was the medicinal powder. At least he had something to be grateful for. He also had something to look forward to. This was the night he and Jessica were going to the rock-and-roll club. It meant she'd be leaving for Ohio the next day, but tonight she'd be with him.

He got to Cobra Kai, changed into a *gi*, and was ready for his lesson. Silver was on the phone in the office so Daniel began his workout alone. He began with a moment of meditation and then stood up in front of the mirror and started the *kata* he had been working on with Mr. Miyagi.

"What are you wasting your time with *kata* for? Didn't I tell you it's useless in a tournament? Now, come over here and let's get back to learning something that can do some real damage."

Daniel dropped the *kata* position and followed his new *sensei* to the metal rack. Today, a two-by-four was clamped at head level — the same place

Mike Barnes's picture had been the day before.

"Rule number three: A man can't see; he can't fight. Hit him square in the nose. He'll be blinded by tears and choke on his own blood. Make a fist." Daniel folded his knuckles carefully into a fist. "Good. Now, here's what you do. You wait until your enemy is moving forward, and when he's close in, so the action's confused, take him and — *Kiaiiii!*" Silver fired at the board, smashing it in two with his fist.

"See, if he just runs into your fist, well, it's not your fault. He's out and he can't continue. You're the champion. Now you try it." He replaced the smashed board with a fresh one.

It sounded so simple, and, in a way, so logical, but the purpose of combat in a tournament was to score points, not draw blood. Daniel considered Silver's logic and there was no doubt about it: If his opponent couldn't continue because he'd run smack into his fist, Daniel would win.

Daniel aimed and fired. "Ouch!"

"Do it again."

Daniel punched, but the shot wasn't true and his knuckles smashed against the board, noisily and ineffectively.

"Mr. LaRusso, you're not concentrating. Now, let's get with it."

He tried again. This time he concentrated, but he missed. He felt his fear of pain. It was as real as the board that confronted him. He fired at the board again, but he knew that until he overcame the fear, he'd never smash the board. His punches were no more than taunts. He bore down, focusing, concentrating. It took everything he had. He began *kiaii*ing as he struck. With each shot, his cry got louder, his punch got truer.

"Good! Again! Again!" Silver encouraged him. "See it now! This is not a bunch of sticks and pipes. This is a living, breathing, fighting machine that wants to kill. He wants to break you. Humiliate you. Are you going to let this happen?"

"No, sir," Daniel said.

"I can't hear you."

"No, *sir*." He spoke louder. As he spoke, he saw the two-by-four become Mike Barnes. There were Mike's fiery eyes, the sneering curl of his lip — the hatred. It lived.

"And what are you going to do if he tries?"

"Stop him, sir." Daniel spoke rapidly, spitting out the words like a machine gun.

"How?"

"I'll hit him."

"How will you hit him?"

"Hard."

"How?"

"Hard!"

"How?"

"Hard!!"

"How?"

"HARD!!"

"Then do it!" Silver snapped.

Daniel charged the board a final time. This time he was prepared. He swept the footboard with the blade of his foot, smashing it in two. He sliced through the chest-level board with the back of his arm. Finally he slammed the headboard with his fist, punching through the wood as if it were paper.

Silver gleamed. "All right! You're ready!"

"I am ready!" Daniel said, feeling it in his heart, and it was a very good feeling.

He and Silver exchanged high fives. Daniel was careful to use the hand that didn't hurt from punching the wood.

The first thing Daniel saw when he pulled up to the bonsai shop that afternoon was a sign in the window that read *Help Wanted*. He scowled at it and entered, nodding politely to the customers who were carrying out a bonsai tree in the shop's distinctive pot.

"What do we need help for?" Daniel asked.

Mr. Miyagi looked up from the cash register. "*We* don't. I do. The shop is too much for one person to run."

"But I'm here."

"Where?" Mr. Miyagi asked. "This is only the second time in a week, and it's already four-thirty."

What Mr. Miyagi said was true. Daniel had been so busy with his training that he'd hardly had a minute to spare for the shop, but he didn't want it to be that way. "Okay, tomorrow, I'm here. Eight o'clock sharp, on the button, to open up. I promise."

"Tomorrow is Sunday, Daniel-san. We are closed. Remember?"

Daniel looked back at the sign. "So what you're

saying with this is that I don't have to come in at all anymore?"

"That not what I am saying."

"Well, it sure looks like it," he said, waving the sign in Mr. Miyagi's face.

"Then maybe you should get eyes and ears checked if that is what you see and hear."

"There's nothing wrong with my eyes and ears," Daniel said, the anger and hurt welling up inside him.

"Then maybe there's something wrong with your training, Daniel-san, that sends you home bruised and bloodied and angry, and makes you forget your other responsibilities."

Daniel thought he understood then what was at the root of this. "You thought I would quit the tournament because I couldn't do it without you. But now that you see that I *am* doing it without you, you're using the shop to blackmail me!"

Mr. Miyagi started to speak, but Daniel cut him off. "Well, it's not going to work. You can keep the whole shop. I don't care!"

For the second time that week, Daniel stormed out of the shop and into his car, more convinced than ever that all his troubles were Mr. Miyagi's fault.

Chapter 20

Daniel met Jessica outside of the rock-and-roll club, The Downstairs, that night at nine o'clock as they had planned. She seemed almost surprised to see him. Daniel suspected she'd been spending time with Mr. Miyagi when he hadn't been in the shop. It was a safe bet that the old man had told her a lot of things about him that just weren't true. He was confident he'd have a chance to show her that evening that he really was just fine. It was Mr. Miyagi who was going a little off the rails.

"Hey! How are you doing?" he greeted her cheerfully.

"Okay. I didn't know if you'd show up."

"Why not?"

"Well, I saw the Help Wanted sign — "

"Yeah, but let me explain — " Daniel began.

"I know. You're under a lot of pressure . . ."

"But that's no excuse," Daniel said earnestly.

". . . but taking it out on everyone around you is not going to help."

"I know," Daniel conceded. "I've been a little out

of it. I'm going to straighten it all out. Please forgive me. I promise that things are coming together for me with my training and all. In fact, everything's great and I'll be okay. Better than that, really."

Jessica smiled at him. That smile could melt the hardest heart. "Well, then, let's go rock and roll."

"Let's do it," he said, taking her hand and leading the way into the noisy, crowded club.

The music was good. It was just what Daniel and Jessica needed. For Daniel, it was a way to celebrate his progress as Silver's student. For both of them, it was a way to have a night to remember for a long time.

Daniel found that Jessica was as good at dancing as she was at rappeling. They never sat down for the whole forty-five minutes of the band's first set, but when the music stopped, they were ready to.

"If I don't get something to drink, I'm going to die!" Jessica said. Daniel led her over toward the bar. He was surprised when he found himself face-to-face with his *sensei*, Terry Silver.

"Hi. Some band, huh?" Silver said.

"Yeah, they're great. We're going to get something to drink."

"I'll come with you. My treat," Silver offered.

The three of them joined the end of the line at the soda bar and were chatting about the band and the club, when a big guy came out of the crowd and started talking to Jessica.

"Hi," he said, leering at her.

"Hi," Jessica responded, and then turned away to resume talking to Daniel and Silver.

The big guy continued talking to Jessica. "I've been watching you. You're beautiful," he said.

"Excuse me," Daniel interrupted. "She's with me."

"Says who?" the bully demanded.

"I am," Jessica confirmed.

Daniel didn't like the looks of the situation. It was clear the guy was aching for a fight, but it was odd, too. Daniel wondered what made the guy think Jessica would be in the least bit interested in him. Daniel put his arm across Jessica's shoulder and led her up to the soda bar since they were now at the head of the line.

"Hey!" the bully said, grabbing Daniel's shoulder.

Daniel never even thought about what he did. In an instant, he turned and smashed his fist into the guy's face. The guy tumbled backwards and started yelping in pain.

"My nose! He broke my nose!" the guy yowled, covering his bleeding nose with his hands. He fell back down onto the floor.

The crowd became excited, with shouts of "Fight! Fight!"

Daniel was dazed. He looked at his fist, as if to make sure it was attached to his own arm. He'd never done anything like that before in his life. He couldn't believe he'd done it now.

"What's wrong with you?" Jessica asked. There was real anger in her voice. Daniel wanted to explain, but she didn't give him a chance. She turned and ran out the door of the club.

Daniel was going to follow her, but the club's security guards were approaching, and Daniel didn't want to run straight into them. He didn't know what to do.

Silver grabbed him around the shoulders and together they backed into the crowd. "This way," Silver said. He led Daniel through the crowd deftly. They passed by the soda bar and the men's room, entered the kitchen, and exited through the club's rear door.

Suddenly there was welcome silence. Daniel leaned back against the wall of the building and breathed the fresh evening air. He looked at his hand once more, still stunned by events.

"Did you see how it worked?" Silver asked him. "You didn't even think. Something got in your way. Bang! Down it went. Technique and killer instinct. You've got it all now, kid. You're ready."

Daniel couldn't believe the words he was hearing. Killer instinct? That wasn't what karate was about, he knew that. How could he listen to this? What did it mean?

Silver spotted the look of confusion and horror on Daniel's face. "What's the matter?" he asked.

"I've got to go," Daniel said.

"Where?"

"Anywhere."

Daniel stood up and walked away, cupping his deadly fist in his other hand.

Chapter 21

That night, when Daniel got into his car to drive and think, he didn't drive around in circles. He knew what that had gotten him. It was time for some straight driving and some straight thinking. He had things to do, and the first was at Jessica's house.

He knocked on her door. She opened it a crack and spoke to him coldly.

"What do you want?"

"Can I talk to you?"

"I'm busy," Jessica said. Daniel could see her clothes laid out on the bed behind her. She was packing to return to Ohio.

"It'll only take a minute," Daniel assured her. With apparent reluctance, Jessica let him in. "Look, I want to apologize for what happened. It shouldn't have happened."

"Tell that to the guy whose nose you broke."

"That's my next stop. You were my first. I didn't want you to leave thinking that was me."

"Oh? Who was it? Conan the Barbarian?"

"I deserved that. Look, I've been trying to be

98

someone I'm not and it just isn't working. I'm losing control."

"The only thing I see you losing control of is your temper," Jessica said.

"And your friendship and Mr. Miyagi's trust. I'm losing everything. And I'm not sure I know how to stop it."

Daniel could feel Jessica looking at him, trying to understand what he was saying. She sat down in her den and invited Daniel to sit down, too. "Daniel, you're not alone. Just because I got upset with you doesn't mean I'm not your friend anymore. And don't be so quick to write Mr. Miyagi off."

"The way I've treated him, he's probably written me off."

"No, he hasn't. He has faith in you. He loves you."

Daniel didn't think Jessica could know that those were the things Daniel was worried about most.

"Let's see how much faith he has in me after he's heard what I've done."

"Well, I think he'd better hear it from you first."

Daniel knew she was right about that.

"It'll be okay," Jessica said and, for the first time in a long time, Daniel thought it might be true.

"I'm going to miss you," Daniel said.

"I'm going to miss you, too," Jessica said.

"I'm rooting for Elizabeth Anne, you know," he teased.

Jessica smiled, understanding. "You'll be fine without me. Just get to Mr. Miyagi before anybody else does."

Daniel rose to go. "Thanks, friend," he said, reaching out to Jessica. She stepped over to him and gave him a sweet good-bye kiss. He'd remember it for a long time.

Mr. Miyagi was sitting in the garden when Daniel got home. He needed to talk to him, but he wanted to find out how the guy from the club was first. He called the Valley Hospital emergency room. They had no information on somebody with a broken nose, and it didn't sound as if he'd even been there. Daniel didn't know who else to call. He felt bad. The guy had been a rude jerk, but it shouldn't have cost him a broken nose.

Disheartened, Daniel walked out into the garden and sat next to Mr. Miyagi. It was time to clean the whole slate. Mr. Miyagi had heard the phone call. He knew what had happened. Daniel didn't bother him with details. They were unimportant. Friendships were important.

"I've been so angry at you for not teaching me, I didn't stop to think what I was learning."

Mr. Miyagi looked at Daniel and took in the sore, bandaged hand and Daniel's bloodstained shirt. He said nothing. Daniel continued.

"I feel dead inside. I feel like that tree, all broken and twisted. You know — just pulled apart."

Mr. Miyagi turned to Daniel. "Let me show you something," he said standing up. Daniel followed him through the gate and into the house.

Daniel continued talking as they walked. "That

guy, Terry Silver, he's been helping me train for the tournament. I don't know. I'm sure he means well. A lot of things he said sounded right. Maybe I just got it wrong, but I know that I really messed up this time. I feel I hurt you and me and it's never going to heal."

"Everything can heal. It just takes time. And care."

Mr. Miyagi brought Daniel out onto the front porch. There, on the bonsai rack, was the precious natural bonsai, and it was healing. The little tree had a new growth of needles. It was firm and straight in the soil. The broken branch even seemed to have mended. Daniel was astonished.

"Strong roots, I guess," he remarked. "I'm sorry, Mr. Miyagi. When I started out, I never meant it to end up the way it did."

"When you take a trip, always know where you want to end up, Daniel-san. Sometimes it's better just to stay home."

Daniel looked at the man, his partner, his friend. "Boy, it's been lonely without you," he said.

"Been lonely without you, too," Mr. Miyagi said.

Then Daniel knew exactly what he had to do. Nothing was worth risking his friendship with Mr. Miyagi. Not a tournament championship, not a well-meaning *sensei* like Silver. It was time to stop taking that particular trip and stay home with Mr. Miyagi. "Yeah, well, I'm back now and I'm going to stay. I just have to tell Silver I'm dropping out. I won't be long."

"Want Miyagi to go with you?" he offered.

"I got myself in. I'll get myself out. Thanks for being here," Daniel added.

"Where else would I be?" Mr. Miyagi bowed to Daniel.

Daniel climbed into his car and started the engine. He felt good — really good. He was home.

Chapter 22

The workout room of the Cobra Kai *dojo* was dark when Daniel arrived. It wasn't surprising. After all, it was nearly midnight, but Daniel thought he saw a light on in the office.

He parked his car and peered in the window, trying to see if Silver actually was in the office. He knocked on the door. There was no response. Daniel squinted. Then he saw shadows moving. There definitely was someone there. He tried the handle of the door. It opened. Daniel stepped in.

Now he could hear laughter from the office. He hoped he wasn't interrupting anything. "Mr. Silver? You there?" he asked tentatively. "Hello?"

The laughter stopped. Silver emerged from the office and greeted Daniel.

"There you are! Where'd you go?"

"I, uh, had to think about things," Daniel said. He knew he was going to disappoint the *sensei*, but he also knew it was the right thing to do, for him.

"And?" Silver asked expectantly.

"I've decided not to defend the title. I really appreciate everything you've done for me. I just wanted to let you know in person. I figured I owed you at least that."

Silver switched on the lights in the *dojo*. Daniel could see his face clouded with anger. "You owe me a lot more than that, Danny boy."

They had never discussed payment for the lessons. Daniel had hoped Silver was doing it for free, perhaps as more of Kreese's apology, but he realized that might not have been true. "I can pay you for the lessons, Mr. Silver. It'll take a while, but you can have the money. I know they weren't free."

"Nothing's for free," Silver said. "The fee is that you are going to defend your title. You're getting in that ring."

Daniel was surprised at Silver's attitude. He hadn't realized how much it meant to Silver. It was understandable that any *sensei* would want the champion to be his student, but Silver seemed to be implying more than that.

"You can't make me do something I don't want to do," Daniel said.

Silver smiled. Then he laughed, but it wasn't a nice laugh at all. "Danny, Danny, Danny. From the moment you met me, I've been making you do things you didn't want to do."

"What are you talking about?" Daniel asked.

"What am I talking about? Shall we tell him what I'm talking about?" Silver asked, speaking to someone in his office. The action confused Daniel. But when Mike Barnes stepped out of Silver's office, all confusion fled. Daniel understood absolutely everything clearly. It was Terry Silver who was paying Mike Barnes to whip Daniel at the championship. Everything Silver taught Daniel was designed to make him lose.

"We have an agenda here, Daniel," Silver said.

"You guys are crazy."

"So, who isn't?" Mike asked.

"It's very simple," Silver explained. "You either fight on one day, or you fight every day for the rest of your life."

"Which might not be very long," Mike said.

"You guys are sick. You're not going to pull this off," Daniel said, backing away toward the door. He might, just might, have a chance against either Silver or Mike, but there was no way he could beat both of them at once. Every instinct he had told him to get out of there. He spun to exit as fast as possible and found himself looking straight into the oversized chest of a very healthy and very much alive John Kreese.

Kreese laughed and chased Daniel back into the middle of the *dojo*.

"Mike, let's show Mr. Kreese how he's going to get back into business."

"I don't want to fight. You can't make me fight, so forget about it."

"Okay," Silver said coldly. "Just stand there and let him beat you to a pulp."

Mike settled into a fighting stance. It was a perfect setup for a sweep. Daniel swung his leg into motion and gave it everything he had, but Mike shifted his position, swinging his own legs out of

Daniel's range. It knocked Daniel off balance. Before he could fall, Mike charged him and grabbed him by the shirt and belt and rammed him into the nearest wall.

Mike only gave Daniel a second to recover, then he attacked again, punching him mercilessly. "You're doing this to yourself," Mike said.

Daniel answered with punches, but they were easily blocked. Mike tossed him across the room like a pillow. He landed near the door. Stumbling, he tried to reach it, but Mike chased after him and tossed him back into the *dojo*. Daniel waited for the next blow. It didn't come. There was a stunned silence in the *dojo*.

"Look who's here," Silver said.

Mr. Miyagi entered.

"What are you waiting for?" Silver said to Mike. The contender charged at Mr. Miyagi, *kiaii*ing loudly. His blows fell on air, however, because Mr. Miyagi sidestepped them. Mike plowed straight into the wall, headfirst, and was knocked out cold.

"Party time!" Kreese announced, glee in his voice. He charged Mr. Miyagi. Again, Mr. Miyagi sidestepped the attack. He delivered three sharp blows to Kreese as the man stumbled. Kreese was out of the fight.

"All right, old man, let's see how good you are," Silver said, spitting out the words.

Mr. Miyagi was good. He was very good and a lot better than Silver. Within seconds, Silver was trying to shake cobwebs out of his head, along with Kreese and Mike.

"You think this is the end of it?" Silver asked, rubbing his head. "Let me tell you. After my boy wins the title, I'm going to open Cobra Kai *dojos* all over this valley. I might even give lessons for free. From now on, when people say karate around here, the only thing they'll mean is Cobra Kai karate. John Kreese's karate. You won't even be a memory."

Daniel stood up and walked to his friend. "Yes he will," he said, defending Mr. Miyagi. "You are the one who will be forgotten."

"To you, I'll be a memory," Silver said. "I'm in your mind, see. And once I'm in, I don't get out. You're like my little robot. All programmed and ready to roll. Rudy gets you angry. You break his nose. You're mine, Danny boy. Mine."

It only took Daniel a second to see that in one way at least, Silver was right, and it was frightening. If Mike won, whether he beat Daniel or not, Silver would be able to make a fortune opening more *dojos* and ruining the spirit of karate for every youngster who studied his methods.

Daniel turned to Mr. Miyagi. "Now will you train me?"

"*Hai*, Daniel-san. Now I will train you."

As they walked out of the *dojo* together, there were many thoughts on Daniel's mind. In the forefront was the natural bonsai, its new growth coming in green and strong.

Chapter 23

Daniel's training began early the next day. They worked on blocks and evasions, punches, kicks, and strikes, the basic moves of karate combat. They worked on *go* and *ju*, and meditation. Most of all, they worked on the *kata*.

At first, Daniel found himself thinking about the training he knew Mike was doing on the other side of town. He'd be punching, chopping, and kicking at blocks of wood until his hands, arms, and feet were red and swollen and until the wood was splintered. Daniel imagined what it would be like to be on the receiving end of enough force to split a two-by-four.

"Daniel-san," Mr. Miyagi said gently. "No can win tournament by thinking about getting hurt."

Daniel smiled. Mr. Miyagi had an uncanny way of knowing exactly what was on his mind all the time. He returned his thoughts to his own training, starting the *kata* from the beginning.

"Good, Daniel-san," his own *sensei* said. "Always remember, root of karate is in *kata*."

For days, they divided their time between the shop and karate training. As the time passed and the training progressed, Daniel became stronger and faster. He was growing in the way of Miyagi karate and with each workout, found himself farther and farther from the painful memories of the Quick Silver method.

Each day, too, they spent time tending to the natural bonsai. It was remarkable how it recovered from its ordeal. The new needles grew in fresh and strong. Even the damaged branch seemed to have been bonded back to the trunk, for it, too, had needles, and even new growth.

One Sunday, when the shop was closed, the two of them packed ropes and climbing gear and took the bonsai back to Devil's Cauldron.

They secured their ropes and lowered themselves to the indentation in the rocky wall where the bonsai had thrived so long.

Mr. Miyagi placed the tree back where it had been safe and secure and carefully packed the earth around it. They both studied the tree with deep respect. Mr. Miyagi cupped his hands together, as if to bow to the tree. Then he turned to Daniel. "Like tree has strong root, now so do you, Daniel-san. And like tree chooses how it grows, so you too can now choose how you grow. Take what you learn and make it work for you."

"I feel like I don't know anything," Daniel confessed.

"That is always first step to knowing something. I have faith in you."

The old man tugged at his ropes and began his ascent.

Daniel turned to the little tree for a last look. "Sorry," he said, knowing the apology was totally inadequate for the wrong he'd done, but it was all he had. Then, as Mr. Miyagi had done, Daniel cupped his hands and bowed to the tree.

He knew that if he were to come back to that place in another fifty years, the little tree would still be there, growing strong and free. He hoped the same would be true of himself.

Chapter 24

The scene that greeted Daniel and Mr. Miyagi at the tournament was both wonderful and horrible. For Daniel, the wonderful part was the memory of his incredible victory twelve months earlier. The excitement of the crowd, the bright lights, the sounds of karate matches. It brought back a flood of memories.

The horrible part was the spectacle of the Cobra Kai *dojo* contingent. Mike was in the middle of a bout when they entered the arena. He outmatched his opponent by a large degree and could beat him using only half of his skill. Instead, Mike Barnes was pummeling the boy. Silver, Kreese, and the thug who had been accompanying Barnes were standing at the edge of the ring cheering loudly. Some men with them were handing out Cobra Kai T-shirts, a very popular item with the crowd. It dismayed Daniel and Mr. Miyagi to see such a brutal form of the sport being so widely accepted.

Mike's bout ended with his opponent being helped out of the ring by his trainer and his mother — with tears streaming down her face. The referee winced with every step the boy took. Mike beamed with pride and then looked around expectantly. It was time for his match with Daniel.

The announcer turned on his microphone and spoke into it. "Mr. Silver here," he said, pointing to the contingent from Cobra Kai, "has asked me to announce the founding of his new chain of *dojos*, Cobra Kai Incorporated, in partnership with his longtime training mate, *Sensei* John Kreese."

Daniel heard the words. Now he was more certain than ever that his mission was to put them out of business before they opened their doors. He didn't ever want to see another karate match like the semifinal he'd just witnessed.

The announcer spotted Daniel at the edge of the ring. "And now for the match you've all been waiting for. The finals of the Fifteenth Annual All-Valley Karate Championship. In the black, representing Cobra Kai, the challenger, Mike Barnes."

Mike stepped into the ring. There were cheers, but, Daniel noted with pleasure, there were also boos.

"And in this corner, someone who needs no introduction, the defending champion from the Miyagi-do *dojo*, Daniel LaRusso."

There were only cheers for Daniel.

The announcer introduced the referee. The boys met him in the center of the ring.

"This match will have a three-minute time limit. You both know the rules. Light contact to the body is allowed. No contact to the face. Three points wins. Bow."

Daniel bowed. Mike stared at him stonily.

"Bow!" the referee said insistently. Mike nodded his head.

"On guard. Begin."

Instantly Mike charged at Daniel, kicking furiously. Daniel evaded the kicks, but found himself backing out of the ring.

The referee brought them both back to the center of the ring. "On guard. Continue."

They began again, circling each other, each looking for a chance, neither wanting to commit to a technique too early, or give away any strategic information. Then Daniel thought he saw an opportunity and attacked. He swept at Mike's ankles, knocking him to the mat. Daniel kicked again, but this time Mike grabbed Daniel's foot and threw him onto the mat. He was about to attack at the back of Daniel's head when the referee interfered. He gave Mike a brief warning, and then the bout began again.

Mike charged, and this time he landed a punch.

"Point! Barnes!" the referee announced. Daniel rubbed his ribs where Mike had jabbed him. There had been nothing light about the contact, but he hadn't expected any mercy from his opponent.

Mike charged again, but this time Daniel was ready and tripped him. As Mike rose from the mat, Daniel threw a back kick. Mike grabbed Daniel's leg and kicked him in the groin. Daniel hit the deck at the side of the ring. The crowd booed.

"Intentional groin contact," yelled the referee. "Loss of a point. Score is zero to zero. On guard. Continue."

Mike punched at Daniel five times. Daniel avoided all five punches and then double punched Mike. Mike blocked the punches and then pounded Daniel with a series of undercuts.

"Point! Barnes," the referee announced.

Mike raised his arms in triumph.

"On guard. Continue."

Mike threw a spin-back kick. Daniel saw it coming in time and pulled him down. Furious, Mike leapt up and smashed Daniel in the face.

The referee angrily pulled Mike away.

"Face contact. You lose a point, Barnes. One more penalty and you're disqualified." The referee turned to Daniel. "You okay, son?" he asked.

Daniel nodded.

"On guard. Continue."

Mike began to pummel Daniel with blows, kicks, and punches, but no points were made. The blows were blocked or landed without a score. Daniel held on, but he was beginning to feel stunned. The beating he was taking proved that the Quick Silver method was vicious — and effective.

Then, just as Mike began to aim a series of roundhouse kicks at Daniel's weary body, the buzzer sounded.

Daniel slumped to the mat. Above the roar of the crowd he could hear the tournament announcer.

"And with the score tied at zero to zero, regulation time has run out. The fighters will take a one minute time-out. Under the All-Valley Karate Association's rules the match will resume in a sudden-death overtime. The first man to score will be declared the All-Valley Champion."

Chapter 25

Mr. Miyagi approached the spot where Daniel still lay on the mat.

"I can't beat him," Daniel said.

"Must beat him," Mr. Miyagi said simply. "If do not, that is the future of karate in the Valley." He pointed across the ring, where Kreese and Silver were coaching Mike and obviously congratulating him for the vicious beating he was in the process of delivering.

"You've got to give me a secret technique."

"Everything you need, Daniel-san, you have. Remember lesson of natural bonsai. Tree with strong root chooses own way to grow. Like tree, you have strong root. Follow own way. Remember *go ju*. Hard soft."

"Time," the referee announced.

"Good luck," Mr. Miyagi said. Then he added, "Daniel-san, remember all karate is found in *kata*."

Daniel had spent more than a hundred hours working on the *kata*. By the time he'd finished his training, he knew every nuance of every move of the routine. He was one with it, but he couldn't see how he was going to beat a powerhouse like Mike Barnes with a *kata* he'd performed a thousand times by himself.

"Time!" called the referee. "Fighters to your marks."

Mike stood on his mark, dancing, but Daniel did not rise. Suddenly Silver ran out onto the mat.

"That's it. It's over. He can't get up. The winner . . ."

Silver lifted Mike's hand up.

"I'll decide that," said the referee, waving Silver away. "Off the mat."

The referee knelt beside Daniel. "Can you continue, son?" he asked.

Daniel looked up. He saw Mike sneering at him. He heard Silver laugh. Then Daniel looked at Mr. Miyagi, and he knew what his answer had to be.

"Yes."

Daniel rose and approached his mark. The crowd roared in approval.

"On guard. Continue."

Mike lunged, something he'd done a lot of. This time, however, Daniel didn't retreat, he sidestepped. Mike flew past him out of the ring. There were laughs from the crowd.

"Out of bounds."

Mike returned and they started again.

Mike charged again, flailing at Daniel with punches. The sidestep had worked so well Daniel tried it again. It worked again. The crowd laughed some more.

Once again, they began circling. Mr. Miyagi's words came back to Daniel. *Go ju*, hard and soft. Soft karate was based on speed and precision. Hard karate was power and strength. Everything Mike Barnes did was hard karate. He did it well, but it was his only tool. When Daniel tried to fight hard with hard, he lost points. When he used soft karate, sidesteps, ducks, rolls, he made points.

They faced each other for their one-point match. Everything Daniel believed in about karate was on the line now. He had to do it; he *could* do it. Suddenly Daniel was flooded with confidence, and it was a wonderful feeling. Now he was ready for the *kata*.

He began the first movement and as soon as he did it, he knew he was home. The deliberate and careful actions of the *kata* confused Mike. He didn't know what to do as Daniel proceeded confidently.

He tried to find an opening, but even though Daniel was moving slowly, he was moving so surely that Mike was confounded. Daniel stepped forward, Mike shifted back. Daniel spun, Mike looked around in confusion.

"Kill him! Kill him!" was the advice Mike got from his trainers. He lunged at Daniel. At that precise moment, Daniel raised his right arm, easily deflecting Mike's punch and, still following the strict regimen of his *kata*, finished off his opponent with a perfect roundhouse kick. He twisted around and flipped Mike onto his back. The stunned opponent looked up at the ceiling, speechless.

"Point!" the referee shouted, the happiness apparent in his voice. "Winner! Champion!" He lifted Daniel's hand in victory and the crowd, if possible, began cheering even louder.

Daniel's eyes met Mr. Miyagi's. Mr. Miyagi bowed to Daniel. Daniel bowed back at him. Then he hugged Mr. Miyagi, his *sensei*, his partner, and best of all, his friend.

Daniel's victory was sweet, but their accomplishment was greater than that. They had worked together to beat not just Mike Barnes, Terry Silver, or even John Kreese. Surely once and for all, they'd beaten Cobra Kai — the way of the fist.